LOVED

(book #2 in the vampire journals)

Morgan Rice

ISBN: 978-0-9829537-3

Also by Morgan Rice

TURNED
(Book #1 in the Vampire Journals)

FACT:

In Salem, in 1692, a dozen teenage girls, known as "the afflicted," experienced a mysterious illness that led them to become hysterical and to independently scream out that local witches were tormenting them. This led to the Salem witch trials.

The mysterious illness that gripped these teenage girls has never, to this day, been explained.

"She dreamt tonight she saw my statua,
Which, like a fountain with an hundred spouts,
Did run pure blood: and many lusty Romans
Came smiling, and did bathe their hands in it:
And these does she apply for warnings, and portents,
And evils imminent…"

--William Shakespeare, *Julius Caesar*

One

For the first time in weeks, Caitlin Paine felt relaxed. Sitting comfortably on the floor of the small barn, she leaned back against a bale of hay, and exhaled. A small fire raged in the stone fireplace about ten feet away; she had just added a log, and felt reassured by the sound of cracking wood. March wasn't over yet, and tonight had been especially cold. The window on the far wall afforded a view of the night sky, and she could see the snow was still falling.

The barn was unheated, but she sat close enough to the fire for its warmth to take the edge off. She felt very comfortable, and felt her eyes getting heavy. The smell of the fire dominated the barn, and as she reclined a little bit further, she could feel the tension starting to leave her shoulders and legs.

Of course, the real reason for her sense of peace, she knew, was not the fire, or hay, or even the shelter of the barn. It was due to him. Caleb. She sat and stared at him.

He reclined across from her, about fifteen feet away, so perfectly still. He was sleeping, and she took the opportunity to study his face, his perfect features, his pale, translucent skin. She had never seen features so perfectly chiseled. It was surreal, like staring at a sculpture. She couldn't fathom how he had been alive for 3,000 years. She, at 18, already looked older than he did.

But it was more than his features. There was an air about him, a subtle energy that he exuded. A great sense of peace. When she was around him, she knew that everything would be all right.

She was just happy that he was still there, still with her. And she allowed herself to hope that they would stay together. But even as she thought it, she chided herself, knowing that she was setting herself up for trouble. Guys like this, she knew, just didn't stick around. It just wasn't how they were built.

Caleb slept so perfectly, taking such small breaths, that it was hard for her to tell if he was even asleep. He had left earlier, he'd said, to feed. He'd returned more relaxed, carrying a stack of logs, and he'd figured a way to seal the barn door to keep out the snowy draft. He had started the fire, and now that he was asleep, she kept it going.

She reached up and took another sip of her glass of red wine, and felt the warm liquid slowly relax her. She had found the bottle in a hidden chest, under a stack of hay; she'd remembered when her little brother, Sam, stashed it there, months ago, and on a whim. She never drank, but she didn't see the harm in a few sips, especially after what she'd been through.

She held her journal on her lap, page open, a pen in one hand and the glass in the other. She had been holding it for 20 minutes now. She had no idea where to begin. She'd never had trouble writing before, but this time was different. The events of the last several days had been too dramatic, too hard to process. This was the first time she sat still and relaxed. The first time she had felt even remotely safe.

She decided it was best to begin at the beginning. What had happened. Why she was here. Who she even was. She needed to process it. She wasn't even sure if she knew the answers herself anymore.

*

Up until last week, life was normal. I was actually beginning to like Oakville. Then Mom marched in one day and announced we were moving. Again. Life turned upside down, like it always did with her.

This time, it was worse. It wasn't another suburb. It was New York. As in city. Public school and a life of concrete. And a dangerous neighborhood.

Sam was pissed, too. We talked about not going, about taking off. But the truth was, we had nowhere else to go.

So we went along. We both secretly vowed that if we didn't like it, we'd leave. Find someplace. Anywhere. Maybe even try to track down Dad again, though we both knew that wouldn't happen.

And then everything happened. So fast. My body. Turning. Changing. I still don't know what happened, or who I've become. But I know I'm not the same person anymore.

I remember that fateful night when it all began. Carnegie Hall. My date with Jonah. And then...intermission. My....feeding? Killing someone? I still can't remember. I only know what they told me. I know that I did something that night, but it's all a blur. Whatever I did, it still sits like a pit in my stomach. I'd never want to harm anyone.

The next day, I felt the change in myself. I was definitely becoming stronger, faster, more sensitive to light. I smelled things, too. Animals were acting strangely around me, and I felt myself acting strangely around them.

And then there was mom. Telling me she's not my real mom, and then getting killed by those vampires, the ones who'd been after me. I never would've wanted to see her hurt like that. I still feel like it's my fault. But with everything else, I just can't let myself go there. I've got to focus on what's before me, what I can control.

There was my getting caught. Those awful vampires. And then, my escape. Caleb. Without him, I'm sure they would have killed me. Or worse.

Caleb's coven. His people. So different. But vampires, all the same. Territorial. Jealous. Suspicious. They cast me out, and they gave him no choice.

But he chose. Despite everything, he chose me. Again, he saved me. He risked it all for me. I love him for that. More than he'll ever know.

I have to help him back. He thinks I'm the one, some kind of vampire messiah or something. He's convinced I'll lead him to some kind of lost sword, that will stop a vampire war and save everybody. Personally, I don't believe it. His own people don't believe it. But I know that's all he has, and that it means the world to him. And he risked everything for me, and it's the least I can do. For me, it's not even about the sword. I just don't want to see him go.

So I'll do whatever I can. I've always wanted to try to find my dad, anyway. I want to know who he really is. Who I really am. If I'm really half vampire, or half human, or whatever. I need answers. If nothing else, I need to know what I'm becoming…

*

"Caitlin?"

She woke in a daze. She looked up to see Caleb standing over her, hands resting gently on her shoulder. He smiled.

"I think you fell asleep," he said.

13

She looked around, saw her open journal on her lap and snapped it closed. She felt her cheeks flush, hoping he hadn't read any of it. Especially the part about her feelings for him.

She sat up and rubbed her eyes. It was still night, and the fire was still going, although it was down to embers. He must have just woken, too. She wondered how long she had been asleep.

"Sorry," she said. "It's the first I've slept in days."

He smiled again, and crossed the room towards the fire. He threw several more logs on, and they crackled and hissed, as the fire grew greater. She felt the warmth reaching her feet.

He stood there, staring down at the fire, and his smile slowly faded as he seemed to become lost in his thoughts. As he looked into the flames, his face was lit with a warm glow, making him look even more attractive, if that were possible. His large, light brown eyes opened wide, and as she watched him, they changed color to a light green.

Caitlin sat up straighter, and saw that her glass of red wine was still full. She took a sip, and it warmed her. She hadn't eaten in a while, and went right to her head. She saw the other plastic glass sitting there, and she remembered her manners.

"Can I pour you some?" she asked, then added, nervously, "that is, I mean, I don't know if you drink—"

He laughed.

"Yes, vampires drink wine, too," he said with a smile, and came over and held the glass while she poured.

She was surprised. Not by his words, but by his laugh. It was soft, elegant, and seemed to fade smoothly into the room. Like everything else about him, it was mysterious.

She looked up into his eyes as he raised the glass to his lips, hoping that he would look back into hers.

He did.

Then they both looked away at the same time. She felt her heart race faster.

Caleb walked back to his spot, sitting on the straw, leaning back, and looking at her. Now he seemed to be studying her. She felt self-conscious.

She unconsciously ran her hand along her clothing, and wished she were wearing something prettier. Her mind raced as she tried to remember what she had on. Somewhere along the way, she couldn't remember where, they had stopped briefly in some town, and she had gone to the only store they had—a Salvation Army—and found a change of clothes.

She looked down in dread, and didn't even recognize yourself. She wore torn, faded jeans, sneakers a size too big for her, and a sweater over a tee shirt. Over that, she had on a faded, purple pea coat, one button missing, also too big on her. But it was warm. And right now, that was what she needed.

She felt self-conscious. Why did he have to see her like this? It was just her luck that the first time she met a guy she really liked, she didn't even have a chance to make herself look nice. There was no bathroom in this barn, and even if there were, she had no makeup on her. She looked away again, feeling embarrassed.

"Was I sleeping a long time?" she asked.

"I'm not sure. I just woke myself," he said, leaning back and running his hand through his hair. "I fed early tonight. It threw me off."

She looked at him.

"Explain it to me," she said.

He looked at her.

"Feeding," she added. "Like, how does it work? Do you…kill people?"

"No, never," he said.

The room fell quiet as he collected his thoughts.

"Like everything in the vampire race, it's complicated," he said. "It depends on the type of vampire you are, and the coven you belong to. In my case, I only feed on animals. Deer, mostly. They are overpopulated, anyway, and humans hunt them, too—and not even to eat."

His expression turned dark.

"But other covens are not so gracious. They will feed on humans. Usually, undesirables."

"Undesirables?"

"Homeless, drifters, prostitutes…those who won't be noticed. That's the way it's always been. They don't want to draw attention to the race.

"That is why we consider my coven, my breed of vampire, to be pure blooded, and other types to be impure. What you feed on…it's energy infuses you."

Caitlin sat there, thinking.

"What about me?" She asked.

He looked at her.

"Why do I want to feed sometimes, but not others?"

He furrowed his brow.

"I'm not sure. It is different with you. You are a half breed. It is a very rare thing.…I do know that you are coming-of-age. With others, they are turned, overnight. For you, it is a process. It may take time for you to settle, to go through whatever changes you are."

Caitlin thought back and remembered her hunger pangs, how they'd overwhelmed her out of nowhere. How they'd made her unable to think of anything but feeding. It was horrible. She dreaded it happening again.

"But how do I know when it will happen again?"

He looked at her. "You don't."

"But I never want to kill a human," she said. "Ever."

"You don't have to. You can feed on animals."

"But what if it happens when I'm stuck somewhere?"

"You will need to learn to control it. It takes practice. And willpower. It is not easy. But it is possible. You can control it. It is what every vampire goes through."

Caitlin thought about what it would be like to capture and feed on a live animal. She knew she was already faster than she'd ever been, but she didn't know if she was *that* fast. And she wouldn't even know what to do if she actually caught a deer.

She looked at him.

"Will you teach me?" she asked, hopefully.

He met her stare, and she could feel her heart beating.

"Feeding is a sacred thing in our race. It is always done alone," he said, softly and apologetically. "Except..." He trailed off.

"Except?" she asked.

"In matrimonial ceremonies. To bind husband and wife."

He looked away, and she could see him shift. She felt the blood rush to her cheek, and suddenly the room became very warm.

She decided to let it go. She had no hunger pangs now, and she could cross that path when she came to it. She hoped he would be by her side then.

Besides, deep down, she didn't really care that much about feeding, or vampires, or swords, or any of it. What she really wanted to know was about *him*. Or, really, how he felt about her. There were so many questions she wanted to ask him. *Why did you risk it all for me? Was it just to find the sword? Or was it something else? Once you find your sword, will you still stay with me? Even though romance with a human is forbidden, would you ever cross the line for me?*

But she was afraid.

So, instead, she simply said: "I hope we find your sword."

Lame, she thought. *Is that the best you can do? Can't you ever get the courage to say what you're thinking?*

But his energy was too intense, and whenever she was around him, it made it hard for her to think clearly.

"As do I," he responded. "It is no ordinary weapon. It has been coveted by our kind for centuries. It is rumored to be the finest example of Turkish sword ever crafted, made of a metal that can kill all vampires. With it, we'd be invincible. Without it…"

He trailed off, apparently afraid of voicing the consequences.

Caitlin wished Sam was here, wished he could help lead them to her dad. She surveyed the barn again. She didn't see any recent signs of him. She wished, again that she hadn't lost her cell on the way. It would have made life so much easier.

"Sam always used to crash here," she said. "I was sure he'd be here. But I know he came back to this town—I'm sure of it. He wouldn't go anywhere else. Tomorrow we'll go to school, and I'll talk to my friends. I'll find out."

Caleb nodded. "You believe he knows where your father is?" he asked.

"I…don't know," she answered. "But I know that he knows a lot more about him than me. He's been trying to find him forever. If anyone knows anything, it's him."

Caitlin thought back and remembered all those times with Sam, his always searching, showing her new leads, always getting disappointed. All the nights he'd go to his room and sit on the edge of her bed. His desire to see their father had been overwhelming, like a living thing inside of him. She felt it, too, but not as badly as he. In some ways, his disappointment had been harder to watch.

Caitlin thought of their messed-up childhood, of all that they'd missed, and suddenly felt overcome by emotion. A tear formed at the corner of her eye, and, embarrassed, she wiped it away quickly, hoping Caleb hadn't seen.

But he had. He looked up and watched her, intensely.

He got up slowly and sat beside her. He was so close, she could feel his energy. It was intense. Her heart started to pound.

He gently ran a finger through her hair, pushing it back off her face. Then he ran it along the corner of her eye, and then down her cheek.

She kept her face down, staring at the floor, afraid to meet his eyes. She could feel them examining her.

"Don't worry," he said, his soft, deep voice putting her completely at ease. "We will find your father. We'll do it together."

But that wasn't what she was worried about. She was worried about him. Caleb. Worried about when he would leave her.

If she faced him, she wondered if he would kiss her. She was dying to feel the touch of his lips.

But she was afraid to turn her head.

It felt like hours passed until she finally summoned the courage to turn.

But he had already turned away. He was leaning gently back against the hay, eyes closed, asleep, a gentle smile on his face, lit by the firelight.

She slid closer to him and leaned back, resting her head inches away from his shoulder. They were almost touching.

And almost was enough for her.

TWO

Caitlin slid back the door to the barn and squinted at a world covered in snow. White sunlight bounced off of everything. She brought her hands to her eyes, feeling a pain she had never quite experienced: her eyes were absolutely killing her.

Caleb stepped out beside her, as he was finishing wrapping his arms and neck in a thin, clear material. It almost looked like Saran wrap, but it seemed to dissolve in his skin as he put it on. She couldn't even tell it was there.

"What's that?"

"Skin wrap," he said, looking down as he wrapped it carefully again and again over his arms and shoulders. "It's what allows us to go out in the sunlight. Otherwise, our skin would burn." He looked her over. "You don't need it—yet."

"How do you know?" she asked.

"Trust me," he said, grinning. "You'd know."

He reached into his pocket and pulled out a small canister of eye drops, leaned back and put several drops in each eye. He turned and looked at her.

It must have been obvious that her eyes hurt, because he gently placed his hand on her forehead. "Lean back," he said.

She leaned back.

"Open your eyes," he said.

As she did, he reached over and put one drop in each eye.

It stung like crazy, and she closed her eyes and lowered her head.

"Ow," she said, rubbing her eyes. "If you're mad at me, just tell me."

He grinned. "Sorry. It burns at first, but you'll get used to it. Your sensitivity will go away within a few seconds."

She blinked and rubbed her eyes. Finally, she looked up, and her eyes felt great again. He was right: all the pain had gone away.

"Most of us still won't venture out during sunlight hours if we don't have to. We are all weaker during the daytime. But sometimes, we must."

He looked at her.

"This school of his," he said. "Is it far?"

"Just a short walk," she said, taking his arm and leading him across the snowy lawn. "Oakville high. It was my school, too, until a few weeks ago. One of my friends *has* to know where he is."

*

24

Oakville High looked exactly as Caitlin remembered. It was surreal to be back here. Looking up at it, she felt as if she had just taken a brief vacation, and was now back to normal life. She even let herself believe, for a brief second, that the events of the past few weeks had all just been a crazy dream. She let herself fantasize that all was completely normal again, just as it had been. It felt good.

But when she looked over and saw Caleb standing beside her, she knew that nothing was normal. If there was anything more surreal than coming back here, it was returning with Caleb by her side. She would be entering her old school with this gorgeous man by her side, well over six feet, with wide, broad shoulders, dressed in all black, the high collars of his black leather trench coat hugging his neck, slipping under his longish hair. He looked like he had just walked off the cover of one of those popular teenage girl magazines.

Caitlin imagined what the reaction would be when the other girls saw her with him. She smiled at the thought. She had never been especially popular, and certainly no guys had paid much attention to her. She wasn't unpopular—she had some good friends—but she was hardly in the center of the most popular clique, either. She guessed she was somewhere in the middle. Even so, she remembered feeling scorned by some of the more popular girls, who all seemed to stick together, to walk down the halls with their noses up, ignoring anyone they didn't consider to be as perfect as they were. Now, maybe, they would take notice.

Caitlin and Caleb walked up the steps and through the wide double doors to the school. Caitlin glanced at the large clock: 8:30. Perfect. The first class would just be letting out, and the halls would fill any second. That would make them less conspicuous. She wouldn't have to worry about security, or a hall pass.

On cue, the bell rang, and within seconds, the halls started to fill.

The good thing about Oakville was that it was a world apart from that awful New York City high school. Here, even when the halls filled up, there was still plenty of space to maneuver. Large glass windows lined all the walls, letting in light and sky, and you could see trees everywhere you went. It was almost enough to make her miss it. Almost.

She'd had enough of school. She was technically only a few months away from graduation, but she felt as if she'd learned more in the last few weeks than she ever would by sitting in a classroom for a few more months and getting an official diploma. She loved to learn, but she'd be just as happy to never go back again.

As they walked down the hall, Caitlin scanned for familiar faces. They were passing mostly sophomores and juniors, and she didn't spot anyone from her senior class. But as they passed the other kids, she was surprised to see the reaction on all the girls' faces: every single girl literally stared at Caleb. Not a single girl tried to hide it, or was even able to look away. It was incredible. It was as if she were walking down the hall with Justin Bieber.

Caitlin turned and saw that all the girls had stopped, still watching. Several were whispering to each other.

She looked over at Caleb, and wondered if he'd noticed. If he did, he didn't show any sign of it, and he certainly didn't seem to care.

"Caitlin?" came a shocked voice.

Caitlin turned and saw Luisa standing there, one of the girls she'd been friends with before she moved.

"Oh my God!" Luisa added excitedly, throwing her arms wide for a hug. Before Caitlin could react, Luisa was embracing her. Caitlin hugged her back. It felt good to see a familiar face.

"What happened to you?" Luisa asked, speaking in an excited rush, as she always did, her slight Hispanic accent coming through, as she had only moved here from Puerto Rico a few years before. "I'm so confused! I thought you moved!? I texted and IM-ed you, but you never responded —"

"I'm so sorry," Caitlin said. "I lost my phone, and I haven't been near any computers, and—"

Luisa wasn't listening. She had just noticed Caleb, and she was staring, mesmerized. Her mouth literally dropped open.

"Who's your friend?" she finally asked, almost in a whisper. Caitlin smiled: she had never seen her friend so flustered before.

"Luisa, this is Caleb," Caitlin said.

"A pleasure," Caleb said, smiling down, extending his hand.

Luisa just kept staring. She slowly raised her hand, in a daze, obviously too shocked to speak. She looked over at Caitlin, not understanding how Caitlin could have snagged such a guy. She looked at Caitlin differently, almost as if she didn't even know who she was.

"Um…" Luisa began, wide-eyed, "…um…like…where…like…how did you guys meet?"

For a second, Caitlin toyed with how to respond. She imagined telling Luisa everything, and smiled at the thought. That wouldn't work.

"We met…after a concert," Caitlin said.

It was at least partially true.

"OMG, what concert? In the city? The Black Eyed Peas!?" she asked in a rush, "I'm so jealous! I've been dying to see them!"

Caitlin smiled at the thought of Caleb at a rock concert. Somehow, she didn't quite picture him there.

"Um....not exactly," Caitlin said. "Luisa, listen, sorry to cut you off, but I don't have much time. I need to know where Sam is. Have you seen him?"

"Of course. Everybody did. He came back last week. He looked weird. I asked him where you were and what his deal was but he wouldn't tell me. He's probably crashing out at that empty barn he loves."

"He's not," Caitlin answered. "We were just there."

"Really? Sorry. I don't know. He's a sophomore, you know? We don't really cross paths that much. Have you tried IM-ing him? He's always on Facebook."

"I haven't had my phone—" Caitlin began.

"Take mine," Luisa interrupted, and before she could finish, thrust her cell into Caitlin's hand.

"Facebook's already open. Just log in and message him."

Of course, Caitlin thought. *Why didn't I think of that?*

Caitlin logged in, type Sam's name in the search box, brought up his profile, and clicked message. She hesitated, wondering exactly what to write. Then she typed: "Sam. It's me. I'm at the barn. Come meet me. ASAP."

She clicked *send* and handed the phone back to Luisa.

Caitlin heard a commotion, and turned.

A group of the most popular senior girls were heading down the hall, right towards them. They were whispering. And all looking directly at Caleb.

For the first time, Caitlin felt a new emotion well up inside of her. Jealousy. She could see in their eyes that these girls, who never paid her any attention before, would love to steal Caleb away in a second. These girls had sway over any guy in school, any guy they wanted. It didn't matter if he had a girlfriend or not. You just hoped that they didn't set their eyes on *your* guy.

And now they were all staring at Caleb.

Caitlin hoped, prayed, that Caleb would be immune to their powers. That he would still like her. But as she thought about it, she couldn't understand why he would. She was so average. Why would he stick with her when girls like these would die to have him?

Caitlin silently prayed that the girls would just keep walking. Just this once.

But, of course, they didn't. Her heart pounded as the group turned and headed right for them.

"Hi Caitlin," one of the girls said to her, in a fake-nice voice.

Tiffany. Tall, with straight blonde hair, blue eyes, and stick thin. Decked out from head to toe in designer apparel. "Who's your friend?"

Caitlin didn't know what to say. Tiffany, and her friends, had never given Caitlin the time of day. They had never even so much as looked her way. She was shocked that they even knew she existed, and knew her name. And now they were initiating conversation. Of course, Caitlin knew it had nothing to do with her. They wanted Caleb. Badly enough to have to humble themselves to talk to her.

This didn't bode well.

Caleb must've sensed Caitlin's unease, because he took a step closer to her and put one arm around her shoulder.

Caitlin had never been more grateful for any gesture in her life.

With a newfound confidence, Caitlin found the strength to speak. "Caleb," she answered.

"So, like, what are you guys doing here?" another girl asked. Bunny. She was a replica of Tiffany, except brunette. "I thought you, like, left or something."

"Well, I'm back," Caitlin answered.

"So, are you, like, new here, too?" Tiffany asked Caleb. "Are you a senior?"

Caleb smiled. "I am new here, yes," he answered cryptically.

Tiffany's eyes lit up, as she interpreted it to mean he was new to their school. "Great," she said. "There's like a party tonight, if you want to come. It's at my house. It's only for a few close friends, but we'd love to have you. And...um...you, too, I guess," Tiffany said, looking over at Caitlin.

Caitlin felt the anger swelling inside her.

"I appreciate the invitation, ladies," Caleb said, "but am sorry to report that Caitlin and I already have an important engagement this evening."

Caitlin felt her heart swell.

Victory.

As she watched their expressions collapse, like a row of dominoes, she had never felt so vindicated.

The girls turned up their noses and slinked away.

Caitlin, Caleb, and Luisa stood there, alone. Caitlin exhaled.

"OMG!" Luisa said. "Those girls never gave the time of day to anyone before. Much less extended an invite."

"I know," Caitlin said, still reeling.

"Caitlin!" Luisa suddenly said, reaching out and grabbing her arm, "I just remembered. Susan. She said something about Sam. Last week. That he was hanging out with the Colemans. I'm so sorry, it just came back to me. Maybe that helps."

The Colemans. Of course. That was where he'd be.

"Also," Luisa continued, in a rush, "we're all getting together tonight at the Franks. You have to come! We miss you so much. And of course, bring Caleb. It's going to be an awesome party. Half the class is going. You *have* to be there."

"Well... I don't know –"

The bell rang.

"I gotta go! I'm so glad you're back. Love you. Call me. Bye!" Luisa said, waving at Caleb, and turned and hurried down the hall.

Caitlin allowed herself to imagine herself back in her normal life. Hanging out with all her friends, going to parties, being in a normal school, about to graduate. She liked how it felt. For a moment, she tried really hard to push all the events of the last week completely out of her mind. She imagined that nothing bad had ever happened.

But then she looked over and saw Caleb, and reality came flooding back. Her life had changed. Permanently. And it would never change back. She just had to accept it.

Not to mention that she had killed someone, and that the police were looking for her. Or that it would only be a matter of time until they caught her, somewhere. Or the fact that an entire vampire race was looking to kill her. Or that this sword she was looking for could save a lot of people's lives.

Life was definitely not what it was, and never would be. She had to just embrace her current reality.

Caitlin put her hand into Caleb's arm, and led him towards the front doors. The Colemans. She knew where they lived, and that would make sense, Sam's crashing there. If he wasn't in school, then he was probably there right now. That's where they'd have to go next.

As they walked out the front doors and into the fresh air, she marveled at how good it felt to be walking out of this high school again—and this time for good.

*

Caitlin and Caleb walked across the Coleman property, the snow on the grass crunching beneath their feet. The house itself wasn't much – a modest ranch set on the side of a country road. But way back behind it, at the end of the property, it had a barn. Caitlin saw all the beat-up pickup trucks parked haphazardly on the lawn, and could see the footprints in the ice and snow, and she knew a lot of traffic had headed towards that barn.

That was what kids did in Oakville – they hung out in each other's barns. Oakville was as rural as it was suburban, and it gave them the chance to hang in a structure far enough from your parents' house so that they didn't know or didn't care what you were doing. It was a whole lot better than hanging out in the basement.

Your parents couldn't hear a thing. And you had your own entrance. And exit.

Caitlin took a deep breath as she walked up to the barn and slid back the heavy, wooden door.

The first thing that hit her was the smell. Pot. Clouds of it hung in the air.

That, mixed with the smell of stale beer. Way too much of it.

Then what struck her—more than everything else—was the smell of an animal. She had never had such keen senses before. The shock of this animal's presence raced through her senses, as if she had just sniffed ammonia.

She looked to her right and zoomed in. There, in the corner, was a large Rottweiler. He sat up slowly, stared at her, and snarled. He broke into a low, guttural growl. It was Butch. She remembered him now. The Colemans' nasty Rottweiler. As if the Colemans needed a vicious animal to add to their picture of mayhem.

The Colemans had always been bad news. Three brothers—17, 15, and 13—somewhere along the way, Sam had become friends with the middle brother, Gabe. Each was worse than the next. Their dad had left them a long time ago, no one knew where, and their mom was never around. They basically raised themselves. Despite their ages, they were always drunk or stoned, and out of school more than they were in it.

Caitlin was upset that Sam was hanging out with them. It couldn't lead to anything good.

Music played in the background. Pink Floyd. *Wish You Were Here.*

Figures, Caitlin thought.

It was dark in here, especially coming from such a bright day, and it took her eyes several seconds to fully adjust.

There he was. Sam. Sitting in the middle of that worn-out couch, surrounded by a dozen boys. Gabe on one side and Brock on the other.

Sam was hunched over a bong. He had just finished inhaling, and he set it down and leaned back, sucking in the air and holding it way too long. He finally released it.

Gabe tapped him, and Sam looked up. In a stoned haze, he stared at Caitlin. His eyes were bloodshot.

Caitlin felt a pain rip through her stomach. She was beyond disappointed. She felt like it was all her fault. She thought back to the last time they saw each other, in New York, to their fight. Her harsh words. *"Just go!"* she had yelled. Why had she had to have been so harsh? Why couldn't she have had a chance to take it back?

Now it was too late. If she had chosen different words, maybe things would be different right now.

She also felt a wave of anger. Anger at the Colemans, anger at all the boys in this barn who sat around on those beat-up couches and chairs, on piles of hay, all sitting around, drinking, smoking, doing nothing with their lives. They were free to do nothing with their lives. But they weren't free to drag Sam into it. He was better than them. He'd just never had any guidance. Never had any father figure, any kindness from their mom. He was a great kid, and she knew that he could be the top of his class right now if only he'd had even a semi-stable home. But at some point, it was too late. He'd just stopped caring.

She took several steps closer to him. "Sam?" she asked.

He just stared back, not saying a word.

It was hard to see what was in that stare. Was it the drugs? Was he pretending not to care? Or did he really not care?

His look of apathy hurt her more than anything. She had anticipated his being so happy to see her, his getting up and giving her a hug. Not this. He didn't seem to even care. As if she were a stranger. Was he just acting cool in front of his friends? Or had she really screwed things up for good this time?

Several seconds passed, and finally, he looked away, handing the bong off to one of his friends. He kept looking at his other friends, ignoring her.

"Sam!" she said, much louder, her face flushing with anger. "I'm talking to you!"

She heard the snickers of his loser friends, and she felt the anger rising up in waves in her body. She was beginning to feel something else. An animal instinct. The anger in her was welling to a point where it was almost beyond control, and she feared that it would soon cross the line. It was no longer human. It was becoming animal.

These boys were big, but the power rising in her veins told her that she could handle any of them in an instant. She was having a hard time containing her anger, and she hoped she would be strong enough to do so.

At the same time, the Rottweiler ratcheted up his growling, as he started slowly walking towards her. It was as if he sensed something coming.

She felt a gentle hand on her should. Caleb. He was still there. He must've sensed her anger rising, the animal instinct between them. He was trying to calm her, to tell her to control herself, not to let herself go. His presence reassured her. But it wasn't easy.

Sam finally turned and looked at her. There was defiance in his look. He was still mad. That was obvious.

"What do you want?" he snapped.

"Why aren't you in school?" was the first thing she heard herself say. She wasn't exactly sure why she said that, especially with all the other things she wanted to ask him. But the motherly instinct in her kicked in. And that was what came out.

More snickers. Her anger rose.

"What do *you* care?" he said. "You told me to go."

"I'm sorry," she said. "I didn't mean it."

She was glad she had a chance to say it.

But it didn't seem to sway him. He just stared.

"Sam, I need to talk to you. In private," she said.

She wanted to get him out of that environment, into the fresh air, alone, where they could really talk. She not only wanted to know about their Dad; she also just wanted to talk to him, like they used to. And to break the news about their Mom. Gently.

But it wasn't going to happen. She could see that now. Things were spiraling downward. She felt that the energy in this crowded barn was just too dark. Too violent. She could feel herself losing control. Despite Caleb's hand, she just couldn't stop whatever was overcoming her.

"I'm all set here," Sam said.

She could hear more snickering among his friends.

"Why don't you relax?" one of the guys said to her. "You're so high strung. Come sit. Take a hit."

He held the bong out to her.

She turned and stared at him.

"Why don't you shove that bong up your ass?" she heard herself say, through gritted teeth.

A chorus of heckling came from the group of boys. "Oh, SNAP!" one of them yelled.

The boy who'd offered her the hit, a big, muscular guy who she knew had been kicked off the football team, turned bright red.

"What'd you say to me, bitch?" he said, standing.

She looked up. He was much taller than she remembered, at least 6' 6". She could feel Caleb's grip on her shoulder tighten. She didn't know whether it was because he was urging her to keep calm, or because he was tensing up himself.

The tension in the room rose dramatically.

The Rottweiler crept closer. He was now only feet away. And growling like crazy.

"Jimbo, relax," Sam said to the big kid.

There was protective Sam. No matter what, protective of her. "She's a pain in the ass, but she didn't mean it. She's still my sister. Just chill."

"I *did* mean it," Caitlin yelled, angrier than ever. "You guys think you're so cool? Getting my little brother high? You're all a bunch of losers. You're going nowhere. You want to mess your own lives, go ahead, but don't drag Sam into it!"

Jimbo look even angrier, if possible. He took a few threatening steps towards her.

"Well look who it is. Miss teacher. Miss mommy. Here to tell us all what to do!"

A chorus of laughter.

"Why don't you and your faggot boyfriend here come make me!"

Jimbo stepped closer and reached up with his big paw of a hand, and pushed Caitlin on the shoulder.

Big mistake.

The anger exploded inside of Caitlin, beyond anything she could control. The second that Jimbo's finger touched her, she reached up with lightning speed, took his wrist, and twisted it back. There was a loud crack as his wrist broke.

She raised his wrist high behind his back, and shoved him, face first, into the ground.

In less than a second, he was on the ground, on his face, helpless. She stepped up and put her foot on the back of his neck, holding it firmly on the floor.

Jimbo screamed out in pain.

"Jesus Christ, my wrist, my wrist! Fucking bitch! She broke my wrist!"

Sam stood up, as did all the others, staring, shocked. He seemed really shocked. How his little sister could have taken down such a huge guy, and so fast, he had no idea.

"Apologize," Caitlin snarled at Jimbo. She was shocked at the sound of her own voice. It sounded guttural. Like an animal.

"I'm sorry. I'm sorry, I'm sorry!" Jim yelled, whimpering.

Caitlin wanted to just let him go, let it be over with, but a part of her just couldn't do it. The rage had overcome her too suddenly, too strongly. She just couldn't let it go. It was still continuing to course, to build. She wanted to kill this boy. It was beyond reason, but she really did.

"Caitlin!?" Sam yelled. She could hear the fear in his voice. "Please!"

But Caitlin couldn't let go. She was really going to kill this boy.

At that moment, she heard a snarl, and out of the corner of her eye, she saw the dog. It leapt, in midair, its teeth aimed right for her throat.

Caitlin reacted instantly. She let go of Jimbo and in one motion, caught the dog in midair. She got under him, grabbed hold of his stomach, and threw him.

He went flying through the air, ten feet, twenty, with such force that he went across the room and through the wooden wall of the barn. The wall cracked with a splintering noise, as the dog yelped and went flying out the other side.

Everyone in the room stared at Caitlin. They couldn't process what they'd just witnessed. It had clearly been an act of superhuman strength and speed, and there was no possible explanation for it. They all stood there, mouths agape, staring.

Caitlin felt overwhelmed with emotion. Anger. Sadness. She didn't know what she felt, and she didn't trust herself anymore. She couldn't speak. She had to get out of there. She knew Sam wouldn't come. He was a different person now.

And so was she.

THREE

Caitlin and Caleb walked slowly along the bank of the river. This side of the Hudson was neglected, littered with abandoned factories and fuel depots no longer in use. It was desolate down here, but peaceful. As she looked out, Caitlin saw huge chunks of ice floating down the river, slowly separating on this March day. Their delicate, subtle cracking noise filled the air. They looked otherworldly, reflecting the light in the strangest way, as a slow mist rose. She felt like just walking out onto one of those huge slabs of ice, sitting down, and letting it take her wherever it went.

They walked in silence, each in their own world. Caitlin felt embarrassed that she had shown such a display of rage in front of Caleb. Embarrassed that she'd been so violent, that she couldn't control what was happening to her.

She was also embarrassed by her brother, that he'd acted the way he did, that he was hanging out with such losers. She had never seen him act like that before. She was embarrassed she had subjected Caleb to it.

Hardly a way for him to meet her family. He must think the worst of her. That, more than anything, really hurt her.

Worst of all, she was afraid where they would go from here. Sam had been her best hope in finding her dad. She had no other ideas. If she did, she would have found him already, herself, years ago. She didn't know what to tell Caleb. Would he leave now? Of course he would. She was of no use to him, and he had a sword to find. Why would he possibly stay with her?

As they walked in silence, she felt the nervousness well up, as she guessed that Caleb was just waiting for the right time to choose his words carefully, to tell her that he had to go. Like everyone else in her life.

"I'm really sorry," she said finally, softly, "for how I acted back there. I'm sorry I lost control."

"Don't be. You did nothing wrong. You are learning. And you are very powerful."

"I'm also sorry that my brother acted that way."

He smiled. "If there is one thing I've learned over the centuries, it is that you cannot control your family."

They continued walking in silence. He looked out at the river.

"So?" she asked, finally. "What now?"

He stopped and looked at her.

"Are you going to leave?" she asked hesitantly.

He looked deep in thought.

"Can you think of any other place your father may be? Anyone else who knew him? Anything?"

She had already tried. There was nothing. Absolutely nothing. She shook her head.

"There must be *something*," he said emphatically. "Think harder. Your memories. Don't you have any memories?"

Caitlin thought hard. She closed her eyes and really willed herself to remember. She had asked herself that same question, so many times. She had seen her father, so many times, in dreams, that she didn't know anymore what was a dream and what was real. She could recite dream after dream where she had seen him, always the same dream, her running in a field, him in the distance, then his getting further away as she approached. But that wasn't him. Those were just dreams.

There were the flashbacks, memories of when she was a young child, going away with him somewhere. Somewhere in the summertime, she thought. She remembered the ocean. And its being warm, really warm. But again, she wasn't sure if it was real. The line seemed to blur more and more. And she couldn't remember exactly where this beach was.

"I'm so sorry," she said. "I wish I had something. If not for your sake, for mine. I just don't. I have no idea where he is. And I have no idea how to find him."

Caleb turned and faced the river. He sighed deeply. He stared out at the ice, and his eyes changed color once again, this time to a sea-grey.

Caitlin felt the time was coming. At any moment he would turn to her and break the news. He was leaving. She was no longer of any use to him.

She almost wanted to make something up, some lie about her father, some lead, only so that he would stay with her. But she knew she couldn't do that.

She felt like crying.

"I don't understand," Caleb said softly, still looking out the river. "I was *sure* you were the one."

He stared out in silence. It felt like hours passed, as she waited.

"And there is something else I don't understand," he said finally, and turned and looked at her. His large eyes were hypnotizing.

"I feel something when I'm around you. Obscured. With others, I can always see the lives we've shared together, all the times that our paths have crossed, in any incarnation. But with you...it's clouded. I don't see anything. That's never happened to me before. It's as

47

if…I'm being prevented from seeing something."

"Maybe we never had any," Caitlin answered.

He shook his head.

"I would see that. With you, I can't see either way. Nor can I see our future together. And that has never happened to me. Never—in 3,000 years. I feel like…I remember you somehow. I feel I am on the verge of seeing everything. It's on the tip of my mind. But it's not coming. And it's driving me crazy."

"Well then," she said, "maybe there's nothing after all. Maybe it's just here, now. Maybe there was never anything more, and maybe there never will be."

Immediately, she regretted her words. There she went again, shooting off her mouth, saying stupid things which she didn't even mean. Why had she had to say that? It was the exact opposite of what she'd been thinking, was feeling. She had wanted to say: *Yes. I feel it, too. I feel like I've been with you forever. And that I will be with you forever.* But instead, it came out all wrong. It was because she was nervous. And now she couldn't take it back.

But Caleb was not deterred. Instead, he stepped closer, raised one hand, and slowly placed it on her cheek, pushing back her hair. He stared deeply into her eyes, and she watched his eyes shift again, this time from gray to blue.

48

They stared deeply into hers. The connection was overwhelming.

Her heart pounded as she felt the tremendous heat rising up all throughout her body. She felt as if she were getting lost.

Was he trying to remember? Was he about to say goodbye?

Or was he about to kiss her?

FOUR

If there was anything that Kyle hated more than humans, it was politicians. He couldn't stand their posturing, their hypocrisy, their self-righteousness. He couldn't stand their arrogance. And based on nothing. Most of them had lived barely 100 years. He'd lived over 5,000. When they talked about their "past experience," it made him physically sick.

It was fate that Kyle had to brush shoulders with them, walk past these politicians every evening, as he rose from his sleep and exited above ground, through their hub at City Hall. The Blacktide Coven had entrenched their habitat deep beneath New York's City Hall centuries ago, and it had always been in close partnership with the politicians. In fact, most of the supposed politicians swarming about the room were secretly members of his coven, executing their agenda across the city, and across the state. It was a necessary evil, this comingling, this doing business with humans.

But enough of these politicians were real humans to make Kyle's skin crawl. He couldn't stand to allow them in this building. It especially bothered him when they got too close to him. As he walked, he leaned his shoulder into one of them, bumping him hard. "Hey!" the man yelled, but Kyle kept walking, gritting his jaw and heading for the wide, double doors at the end of the corridor.

Kyle would kill them all if he could. But he wasn't allowed. His coven still had to answer to the Supreme Council, and for whatever reason, they were still holding back. Waiting for their time to wipe out the human race for good. Kyle had been waiting for thousands of years now, and he didn't know how much longer he could wait. There were a few beautiful moments in history when they had come close, when they had received the greenlight. In 1350, in Europe, when they all had finally reached a consensus, and had spread the Black Plague together. That was a great time. Kyle smiled at the thought of it.

There were a few other nice times, too—like the Dark Ages, when they were allowed to wage all-out war across Europe, kill and rape millions. Kyle smiled wide. Those were some of the greatest centuries of his life.

But in the last several hundred years, the Supreme Council had become so weak, so pathetic. As if they were afraid of the humans.

World War II was nice, but so limited, and so brief. He craved more. There had been no major plagues since, no real wars. It was almost as if the vampire race had been paralyzed, afraid of the growing numbers and power of the human races.

Now, finally, they were coming around. As Kyle strutted out the front doors, down the steps, out City Hall, he walked with a bounce in his step. He increased his stride as he looked forward to his trip to the South Street Seaport. There would be a huge shipment awaiting him. Tens of thousands of crates of perfectly intact, genetically-modified Bubonic Plague. They had been storing it in Europe for hundreds of years, perfectly preserved since the last outbreak. And now they'd modified it to be completely resistant to antibiotics. And it would all be Kyle's. To do with as he wished. To unleash a new war on the American continent. In his territory.

He would be remembered for centuries to come.

The thought of it made Kyle laugh out loud, although with his facial expressions, his laugh looked more like a snarl.

He would have to report to his Rexius, his coven leader, of course, but that was just a technicality. In truth, h would be the one leading it. The thousands of vampires in his own coven—and in all the neighboring covens—

would have to answer to him. He would be more powerful than he ever had been.

Kyle already knew how he would unleash the plague: he would spread one shipment in Penn Station, one in Grand Central, and one in Times Square. All perfectly timed, all at rush hour. That would really get things rolling. Within a few days, he estimated, half of Manhattan would be infected, and within another week, all of them would be. This plague spread quickly, and the way they had engineered it, it would be airborne.

The pathetic humans would cordon off the city, of course. Shut down bridges and tunnels. Close air and boat traffic. And that was exactly what he wanted. They would be locking themselves in to the terror that would follow. Locked in, dying from plague, Kyle and his thousands of minions would unleash a vampire war unlike anything the human race had ever seen. Within a matter of days, they would wipe out all New Yorkers.

And then the city would be theirs. Not just *below* ground, but above ground. It would be the beginning, the siren call for every coven in every city, in every country, to follow suit. Within weeks, America would be theirs, if not the entire world. And Kyle would be the one who started it all. He would be the one remembered. The one who put the vampire race above ground for good.

Of course they would always find a use for the remaining humans. They could enslave those who survived, store them in massive breeding farms. Kyle would enjoy that. He would make sure to get them all plump and fat, and then, whenever his race felt like feeding, they would have an endless variety to choose from. All perfectly ripe. Yes, humans would make good slaves. And quite a delectable meal, if bred properly.

Kyle salivated at the thought. Great times were ahead of him. And nothing would stand in his way.

Nothing, that is, except for that damn White coven, entrenched beneath the Cloisters. Yes, they would be a thorn in his side. But not a major one. Once he found that horrible girl, Caitlin, and that renegade traitor, Caleb, they would lead him to the sword. And then, the White coven would be defenseless. Nothing would be left to stand in their way.

Kyle flared with rage as he thought of that stupid little girl, escaping from his grasp. She had made a fool of him.

He turned down Wall Street, and a passerby, a large man, had the bad fortune of walking his way. As they crossed paths, Kyle bumped his shoulder into him for all he was worth. The man stumbled back several feet, smashing into a wall.

The man, dressed in a nice suit, screamed, "Hey buddy, what's your problem!?"

But Kyle sneered back, and the man's expression changed. At six foot five, with massive shoulders, and huge features, Kyle was not a man to challenge. The man, despite his size, quickly turned and kept walking. He knew better.

Bumping the man made him feel a bit better, but Kyle's rage still flared. He would catch that girl. And kill her slowly.

But now was not the time. He had to clear his head. He had more important things to attend to. The shipment. The wharf.

Yes, he took a deep breath, and slowly smiled again. The shipment was just blocks away.

This would be his Christmas day.

FIVE

Sam woke to a massive headache. He opened one eye, and realized he had passed out on the floor of the barn, in the straw. It was cold. None of his friends had bothered to stoke the fire the night before. They'd all been too stoned.

Worse, the room was still spinning. Sam lifted his head, pulling a piece of straw out of his mouth, and felt an awful pain in his temples. He'd slept in a weird position, and his neck hurt as he twisted it. He rubbed his eyes, trying to get the cobwebs out, but they weren't leaving easily. He had really overdone it last night. He remembered the bong. Then beer, then Southern Comfort, then more beer. Throwing up. Then some more pot, to ease it all out. Then blacking out, somewhere during the night. When or where, he couldn't really remember.

He was hungry but nauseous at the same time. He felt like he could eat a stack of pancakes and a dozen eggs, but also felt like he'd puke the second he did. In fact, he felt like throwing up again right now.

He tried to piece together all the details of the day before. He remembered Caitlin. That, he couldn't forget. It was what really messed him up. Her showing up here. Her taking down Jimbo like that. The dog. What the hell? Did all that really happen?

He looked over and saw the hole in the side of the wall, where the dog had gone through. He felt the cold air rushing in, and knew that it had happened. He didn't really know what to make of it. And who was that dude she was with? The guy look like a NFL linebacker, but pale as hell. He looked like he just stepped out of the Matrix. Sam couldn't even really tell how old he was. The weird thing was, Sam kind of felt like he knew him from somewhere.

Sam looked around and saw all his friends, passed out in various positions, most of them snoring. He grabbed his watch off the floor, saw that it was 11 AM. They'd still be sleeping for a while.

Sam crossed the barn and grabbed a bottle of water. He was about to drink from it, when he looked down and saw it was filled with cigarette butts. Revolted, he set it down, and looked for another. Out of the corner of his eye, he saw a half-empty jug of water on the floor. He grabbed it and drank, and didn't stop drinking until he downed nearly half of it.

That felt better. His throat had been so dry. He took a deep breath, and put a hand on one temple. The room was still spinning. It stank in here. He had to get out.

Sam crossed the room and slid opened the door to the barn. The cold morning air felt good. Thankfully, it was cloudy today. Still bright as hell, though, and he squinted against it. But not nearly as bad as it could've been. And snow was falling again. Great. More snow.

Sam used to love the snow. Especially snow days, when he could stay home from school. He remembered going with Caitlin to the top of the hill and sledding half the day.

But now he mostly skipped school, so it didn't really make a difference. Now, it was just a giant pain in the ass.

Sam reached into his pocket and withdrew a crumpled pack of cigarettes. He put one in his mouth and lit up.

He knew he shouldn't be smoking. But all his friends smoked, and they kept pushing it on him. Finally, he'd said why not? So he started a few weeks back. Now, he was kind of liking it. He was coughing a lot more, and his chest was hurting him already, but he figured, what the hell? He knew it would kill him. But he didn't really see himself living that long anyway. He never had. Somewhere, in the back of his mind, he never really believed he'd make 20.

Now that his head was starting to clear, he thought about yesterday again. Caitlin. He felt bad about it. Really bad. He loved her. He really did. She had come all this way to see him. Why was she asking him about Dad? Had he imagined that?

He couldn't believe she was here, too. He wondered if their mom had freaked out that she'd left. She must've. He bet she was freaking out right now. Probably trying to track them both down. Then again, maybe she wasn't. Who cares? She'd moved them one time too many.

But Caitlin. That was different. He shouldn't have treated her like that. He should have been nicer. He was just too stoned at the time. Still, he felt bad. He guessed there was a part of him that wanted things to go back to normal, whatever that was. And she was the closest thing he had to normal.

Why was she back? Was she moving back to Oakville? That would be awesome. Maybe they could find a place together. Yeah, the more Sam thought about it, the more he really liked the idea. He wanted to talk to her.

Sam whipped out his cell and saw the red light blinking. He pushed the icon, and saw that he had a new Facebook message. From Caitlin. She was at the old barn.

Perfect. That's where he'd go.

*

Sam parked, and walked across the property, to the old barn. The "old barn" is all they had to say. They both knew what that meant. It was the place they always went when they lived in Oakville. It was at the back of a property with a vacant house for sale that had been on the market for years. The house just sat there, empty, asking way too much. Nobody ever even came to look at it, as far as they could tell.

And in the back of the property, way back, there had been this really cool barn, just sitting there, totally empty. Sam had discovered it one day, and had showed it to Caitlin. Neither of them saw the harm in hanging out in it. They both hated their small trailer, being trapped in there with their mom. One night they stayed up late in it, talking, roasting marshmallows in its really cool fireplace, and they both fell asleep. After that, they'd crash in it every now and again, especially whenever things got too crazy at home. At least they were putting it to use. After a few months, they began to feel like it was their place.

Sam walked across the property, a bounce in his step, as he looked forward to seeing Caitlin. His head was really clearing now, especially after that large Dunkin' Donuts coffee he gulped down in the car on the way over. He knew, at 15, he shouldn't be driving. But he was still a couple years away from getting his license, and he didn't want to wait. He hadn't been pulled over yet. And he knew how to drive. So why wait? His friends let him borrow their pickup, and that was good enough for him.

As Sam approached the barn, he suddenly wondered if that big dude would be with her. There was something about the guy...he couldn't quite place it. He couldn't figure out what he was doing with Caitlin. Were they dating? Caitlin had always told him everything. How come he'd never heard of him before?

And why was Caitlin suddenly asking about Dad? Sam was pissed at himself, because there was actually news he'd wanted to tell her. About the other day. He'd finally gotten an answer to one of his Facebook requests. It was their Dad. It was really him. He said he missed them, and wanted to see them. Finally. After all these years. Sam had already responded. They were starting to talk again. And Dad wanted to see him. See them both. Why hadn't Sam just told her? Well, at least he could tell her now.

As Sam walked, snow crunching beneath his boots, snow falling all around him at an increasing rate, he started to feel happy again. With Caitlin around, things might even get back to normal. Maybe she'd showed up at the right time, when he was so messed up, to help snap him out of it. She always had a way of doing that. Maybe this was his shot.

As he reached into his pocket for another cigarette, he stopped himself. Maybe he could turn things around.

Sam crumpled up the pack and threw it in the grass. He didn't need it. He was stronger than that.

He opened the door of the barn, ready to surprise Caitlin and give her a big hug. He would tell her he was sorry. She would be sorry, too, and things would be great again.

But the barn was empty.

"Hello?" Sam called out, knowing, even as he did, that no one was there.

He noticed the dying embers of a fire in the fireplace, one that must have been put out hours ago. But there were no signs of any possessions, of anything that would show they were still there. She'd left. Probably with that dude. Why couldn't she have waited for him? Given him a chance? Even just a few hours?

Sam felt as if someone had just punched him as hard as they could in the gut. His own sister. Even she didn't care anymore.

He had to sit down. He sat on a stack of hay, and rested his head in his hands. He could feel his headache returning. She really did it. She left. Had she gone for good? Deep down, he felt that she had.

Sam finally took a deep breath. All right.

He felt himself hardening up. He was on his own. He knew how to handle that. He didn't need anyone, anyway.

"Hey there."

It was a beautiful, soft, female voice.

Sam looked up, hoping for a second that it was Caitlin. But he already knew, from the second he heard it, that it was not. It was the most beautiful voice he had ever heard.

A girl stood in the entryway to the barn, leaning casually against the wall. Wow. She was stunning. She had long, wavy, red hair, bright green eyes. A perfect body. And she looked about his age, maybe a few years older. Wow. She was *smoking*.

Sam stood.

He could hardly believe it, but the way she stared at him, it looked like she was flirting, like she was really into him. He'd never seen a girl look at him quite like that. He couldn't believe his luck.

"I'm Samantha," she said sweetly, stepping forward and extending one hand.

Sam stepped forward and placed his hand in hers. Her skin was so soft.

Was he dreaming? What was this girl doing here, in the middle of nowhere? How did she even get here? He didn't hear a car pull up, or even hear anyone walking towards the barn. And he'd just got there. He didn't understand.

"I'm Sam," he said.

She smiled wide, revealing perfect, white teeth. Her smile was incredible. Sam felt his knees going weak, as she looked directly at him.

"Sam, Samantha," she said. "I like the sound of that."

He stared back, at a loss for words.

"I saw you out here and figured you must be cold," she said. "Want to come in?"

Sam racked his brain, but couldn't figure out what she meant.

"In?"

"The house," she said, smiling wider, as if that were the most obvious thing in the world. "You know, it has walls and windows?"

Sam tried to comprehend what she was saying. Invite him inside the house? The one that was for sale? Why would she invite him in?

"I just bought it," she said, as if responding to his thoughts. "I didn't have a chance to take down the For Sale sign yet," she added.

Sam was shocked. "You *bought* that house? "

She shrugged. "I had to live somewhere. I'm going to Oakville High. Have to finish my senior year."

Wow. So, that explained it.

So, she was at Oakville. And a senior. Maybe he'd go back to school, too. Hell, yeah. If she was there, why not?

"Yeah, sure, whatever," he said, as casually as he could. "Why not? Love to check it out."

They turned and walked together, back towards the house. As they did, Sam walked passed his crumpled pack of cigarettes, reached down and picked them up. With Caitlin gone, who cared?

"So, then, are you, like, new here?" Sam asked.

He knew it was a stupid question. She'd already told him that she was. But he didn't know what else to say. He was never good at conversation.

She just smiled. "Something like that."

"Why here?" he added. "I mean, no offense, but this town sucks."

"Long story," she said mysteriously.

Something struck him.

"So, like, wait a minute, did you, like, say that you bought the house? As in *you?* Don't you mean your parents?"

"No, I mean me. As in *me*," she answered. "I bought it myself."

He still couldn't understand. He didn't want to sound like an idiot, but he had to figure this out.

"So, like, the house is just for you? Like, your parents—"

"My parents are dead," she said. "I bought it myself. For me. I'm 18 now. I'm an adult. I can do whatever I want."

"Wow," Sam said, genuinely impressed. "That's so cool. A whole house to yourself.

65

Wow. I mean, I'm sorry about your parents, but I…I just don't know anyone like that, like, who owns a house at our age."

She faced him and smiled. "There a lot of surprises you're going to find out about me."

She opened the door and watched as he walked right in, entering the house enthusiastically.

He was so easily led.

She licked her lips, feeling the dull hunger arising in her front teeth.

This was going to be much easier than she'd thought.

SIX

Caleb and Caitlin stood beside the river, staring into each other's eyes. She trembled as she worried if he were about to say goodbye.

But then something caught his eye, and his line of vision suddenly shifted. He looked at her neckline, and seemed transfixed.

He reached out, and she felt his fingers brush her throat. She felt metal. Her necklace. She had forgotten she was wearing it.

He lifted it and stared.

"What is this?" he asked softly.

She reached up and put her hand over his. It was her cross, her small, silver cross.

"Just an old cross," she answered.

But before she'd finished saying the words, she realized: it *was* old. It had been in her family for generations. She hadn't remembered who gave it to her, or when, but she knew it was ancient. And that it had belonged to her father's side. Yes. It was something. Maybe even a clue.

He stared intently, examining it.

"This is no normal cross," he said. "Its edges are curved. I haven't seen one like this for a thousand years. It is the cross of Saint Peter," he stared, mesmerized. "How did you get this?"

"I've…always had it," she said breathlessly, her excitement growing.

"This is the mark of an ancient coven. Of Jerusalem. A secret coven, one of extreme power. It was rumored to not even exist. How do you own this?"

She felt her heart pounding. "I….don't know. I was told it was my father's. I…hadn't even thought of it."

He turned it over gently, looking at the back. His eyes opened wide.

"There is an inscription."

She nodded, suddenly remembering. Yes. There *was* an inscription. What?

"Something in Greek, I think," she said.

"Latin," he corrected. "*Spina rosam et congregari Salem*," he said, and then looked at her, as if expecting her to understand.

She had no idea. She never had.

"It says: *The rose and the thorn meet in Salem.*"

He stared at her, and she stared back.

Her mind raced, wondering what that could mean. His eyes had shone with a newfound purpose.

"This was your father's. It must have been. That inscription is an ancient vampire riddle. He is telling you how to find him. He is telling us where to go next."

She stared back. "Salem?"

He nodded gravely.

He placed a hand on her shoulder. "I care for you greatly. I don't want to see you get hurt. This is my war. I don't want you dragged into it. This will get very dangerous, and you are not a full vampire. You can get hurt. You don't need to come along, especially now that I know where to go next. You have already helped me more than I can thank you for."

Caitlin felt her heart sink. Did he not want her around? Or was he trying to protect her? She felt like it was the latter.

"I know I have a choice," she said. "I choose to be with you."

He stared at her for a long time, then finally nodded. "OK," he said.

"Besides," she added, smiling, "I can hardly let you meet my family alone."

SEVEN

Kyle walked excitedly down the cobblestone streets of the South Street Seaport, doubling his pace. He had pictured this moment for years.

He turned the corner, and he could already begin to see it. The ship. *His* ship.

Disguised as a historic sailing ship on display from a European country, it would be docked at the Seaport for a week. How stupid these humans were. They could believe almost anything. Too trusting to think to check the hull of a piece of history. To realize that it could be the means of their death. Their Trojan horse.

Adding stupidity to stupidity, inane tourists flocked around the ship, delighted to see this piece of history under their noses. If only they knew.

Kyle elbowed his way past the crowds, and headed down an alleyway. Four hulking men stood guard, but when they looked up and saw him coming, they all nodded in recognition and quickly stepped aside. All members of his race. All dressed in black, and as tall as he. Kyle could feel the rage coming off of them to, and it relaxed him. It always felt better to be around his kind.

They parted ways respectfully, and as Kyle walked down the middle, they closed up the alley way again.

Kyle approached the rear of the ship, hidden from the public. Several more of his kind stood by it, and when they saw him approaching, they immediately got to work. They lowered a huge ramp in the side of the hull, and began to wheel down an immense carton, boxed up in plywood. Ten men rolled the massive carton slowly down the ramp, down to the cobblestone sidewalk. Kyle came up to it.

"My master," a short, balding vampire said to Kyle, running up to him and bowing.

This man was sweating profusely, and seemed very nervous. His eyes darted all over the place. He must have been looking out for the police. And it looked as if he had been waiting a long time. Good. Kyle liked to make people wait.

"It is all here," the man continued, in a rush. "We've checked it several times. It's all safe and sound, my master."

"I want to see it," Kyle said.

The man snapped his fingers and four men ran over. They raised crowbars to the carton, and removed one of the wooden planks. They tore away at layer and layers of heavy duty plastic.

Finally, Kyle stepped up and reached in. He felt a cold, glass vial, and extracted it.

He held it up, examining it under the light of a street lamp.

Just as he remembered. Microbes of the bubonic plague swarmed in his hand, perfectly intact. He smiled slowly.

Now his war could begin.

*

Kyle wasted no time. Within hours, he was in Penn Station, ready to get to work. As he marched through the station, against the crowd, his temper flared. He walked right into hordes of people, at rush hour, all racing to get home to their pathetic little families and homes and husbands and wives. He felt his hatred well.

If there was anything he hated worse than a human, it was mobs of them, rushing to and fro in every direction as if their lives mattered even a bit, as if their mere 100 years on this earth held any consequence at all. Kyle had outlived and outlasted them all, generation after generation, for thousands of years. Even the more significant humans, like Caesar and Stalin and—his favorite, Hitler—had been practically forgotten within a few hundred years of their lifetime. They were something at the time, but nothing shortly afterwards. Their frenetic movements, their feelings of self-importance, rattled him to the core. He felt like killing every single one of them. And he would.

But not at this moment.

Kyle had important work to do. *Truly* important work. He was flanked by a small entourage of eight vampire thugs, and they all strutted through the crowd as quickly as possible. Each carried a backpack. And each backpack was packed with 300 vials of the plague. They would split into four teams, and each team, like the four Horsemen, would spread their death to each corner of the station. One team would cover the station itself, one the Path to Grand central, one the A, C, or E subway line, and one the 1 or the 9 train line. Kyle reserved the best location for himself alone: Amtrak. He smiled to think that his portion of the plague would spread farther and wider than any of the others. Just maybe he could take out other cities, too.

Kyle had other vampire minions hard at work, too, in subway stations all over the city, in Grand Central, and in Times Square.

Kyle nodded, and the teams immediately split up. He walked alone towards the Eighth Avenue entrance.

He descended the escalator, walked to the end of the platform, then kept walking, past the point where anyone was looking. He quickly jumped down onto the tracks. As he landed, rats parted ways. They could sense his presence. How ironic, Kyle thought. It was the rats who spread the plague to begin with. Now, they ran from it.

Kyle walked into the blackness, down the tunnel, sticking to the side of the rail. He kept walking, and finally came to the juncture where all the tracks met. He reached into his backpack and took out a vial, and held it up under an emergency light. He could barely contain his excitement. He set down the pack, reached in with both hands, and got to work.

After so many centuries of waiting, it was now only a matter of hours.

EIGHT

Sam couldn't believe his luck. He was being shown around an awesome house by a gorgeous girl—a senior, no less—who seemed into him. She was hot. And really cool. And she had the entire place to herself.

It was like an angel from God had come down and dropped her into his lap. He still couldn't believe it. It was just what he needed, and at just the right time. He was afraid that any second all of his luck would turn, and she'd ask him to leave. But she didn't seem in any rush to ask him to go. In fact, she seemed like she wanted company. And she didn't even care that he'd been in her barn. In fact, she seemed to have liked finding him there. He couldn't believe it. He'd never had any luck in his life like this before.

As he walked around, he saw that her house was still basically empty. No food in the fridge, and not even that much furniture. There was just a random chair here and there, and a small couch. That made him feel good, cause he could help her. If she wanted. He could help her fix it up, move stuff, buy food, shovel, whatever she needed. Even if she just let him crash in her barn, that would be cool. And if she wanted him in the house, well, that would be awesome. More importantly, he really liked her. He was lonely. He realized it now. He really liked being around her.

"And this is the living room," she said, as she walked him into the final room. It was really bare, no pictures on the wall, no rug on the floor—just a small loveseat in the middle.

"Sorry it's still so empty," she said. "I just got here. I didn't want to bring any of my old stuff. I figured I'd just get a new start."

Sam stood there, nodding. He was dying to ask her a whole bunch of questions. Like: *where are you from? How did your parents die? Why did you come here?*

But he didn't want to be too pushy. So he just stood there, nodding, like an idiot.

He also felt kind of nervous. He was really attracted by her, more than he'd been by any girl in his life, and he didn't really know what to say—and didn't trust himself to say anything. He had a feeling that if he said anything, it would come out wrong.

"Want to sit?" she asked, as she walked around and sat in the loveseat.

Do I ever.

He tried not to show his excitement. He tried to walk as casually as he could, as he came over and sat beside her. It was a small loveseat, and his leg brushed up against her as he sat. He could smell her perfume, and he felt his blood race. It was getting hard to think clearly.

She tucked one leg under the other, and turned and faced him. She sat there, smiling, staring into his eyes, and he wondered for the millionth time if this was all a dream, if one of his friends was setting him up for a prank.

"So," she said. "Tell me about you."

"Like what?" he asked.

"Are you from here?"

Sam thought how to answer that one. It wasn't easy.

"No, not really. But I guess you could say I am, since I've lived here more than just about anywhere. We moved around a lot. My family. Well me, my sister, and my mom."

"What about your dad?" she asked immediately.

Sam shrugged.

"He was never around. They said he moved out when I was young. I don't really remember."

"Haven't you tried to track him down?"

Sam looked into her eyes, and wondered if she was able to read his mind.

"It's funny you should ask," he said, "because I actually have been trying. I've always wanted to know. But I never found anything. Until last week."

Her eyes opened wide in surprise. Sam was surprised by how excited she looked. He couldn't really understand it. Why would she care?

"Really?" she asked. "Where is he?"

"Well, I don't know exactly, but we've been talking on Facebook. He says he wants to see me."

"So? Why don't you see him?"

"I want to. It just has all gone down so fast. I guess I just need to make a plan."

"What are you waiting for?" she asked, smiling.

Sam thought. She was right. What *was* he waiting for?

"Why don't you write him back? Make a plan to see him? You know, if you don't set a plan, things never happen. If it were me, I'd message him right now," she said.

Sam looked into her eyes, and as he did, he felt his thoughts shifting. Everything she said made so much sense. It was weird: he almost felt like every time she said something, the thought became his. She was right. He shouldn't wait.

He reached into his pocket, took out his phone, and logged onto Facebook.

As he did, she cuddled up next to him, leaned her shoulder into his, and looked at his phone with him. His heart started racing. He loved the feeling of her shoulder touching his. It was so soft, and fit perfectly. He could smell her hair, and it was overwhelming. He was getting really distracted. He had forgotten, for a second, why he had taken out his phone.

Then he saw the new message light, and opened it.

There it was. Another new message from him.

It read: *Sam, I would love to see you. We do need to get together. I know that you are busy in school and all, but what does your schedule look like? It's hard for me to travel, because of my bad leg, but I'm wondering if you could come up here and visit me? I live in Connecticut.*

Samantha smiled. "There you go," she said.

"What should I say?" Sam asked.

"Say yes. Tomorrow's Saturday. It's the weekend. What better time?"

She was right. Saturday was the best day. Wow. This girl was not only really hot, she was really smart.

Sam typed back: *OK. Sounds good. How about this weekend? What's your address?*

He hesitated for a second. Then he clicked send. He already felt better.

"I'm so excited for you," Samantha said, smiling. "Wow, it's so cool that I could meet you at such an exciting time."

Sam suddenly felt her smooth fingers reach out and stroke his face, then slowly run through his hair. The feeling was intense. Amazing. His heart was slamming, and he could barely think.

He turned and looked at her, and saw that she was facing him, both of her hands now, caressing his face, his neck, his hair. He couldn't pull his eyes away from her large, glowing green eyes. He could hardly breathe.

"I really like you," she said.

Sam opened his mouth to speak, but it was too dry. It took him a couple of tries. "I really like you, too."

He knew he should lean in for a kiss, but he was too nervous. He was relieved when she leaned in, and planted her lips on his.

It was amazing. The blood rushed to his brain, and he prayed this would never end.

NINE

As Caitlin flew with Caleb, arms wrapped around him, loving the feel of his body, she thought of how lucky she was. Just the day before, she'd been worried that Caleb would say goodbye. And now, for once, her luck had changed.

Thank God for that necklace, she thought.

It was late afternoon by the time they arrived in Salem. He set them down inconspicuously in an empty field on the outskirts of town, so no one would notice.

They walked a few blocks, and arrived right on the Main Street of Salem.

Caitlin was surprised. She had expected something more. She'd heard about Salem her whole life, from textbooks mostly, always in connection with the witches. But to see it as a real, living place, as an everyday town, she found quite strange. She had imagined it as a perfectly preserved, historic place in her head, almost like a stage set. To see normal, modern, everyday people living their lives, driving, hurrying to and fro, caught her off guard.

Salem looked almost like any small, New England, suburban town. There were a few chain stores, the typical pharmacies, everything modern, and almost no sign that this town had so much history. The town was also a lot bigger than she had imagined. She had absolutely no idea where to even begin to look for her Dad.

Caleb must've been thinking the same thing at the same time, because he looked over at her with an expression: *what now?*

"Well," she began, "I guess we didn't expect him to be standing on Main Street and waiting to give us a big hug."

Caleb smiled.

"No, I didn't think it would be that easy, either."

"So? Now what?" she asked.

Caleb looked at her. "I don't know," he finally said.

Caitlin stood there, thinking. Several people passed them on the street, and some of them gave Caitlin and Caleb a strange look. She looked at them in the reflection of a store window, and realized that they were a startling couple. They were anything but inconspicuous. He was so tall, and dressed elegantly in all black. He look like a movie star, plopped down in the middle of the street. Standing next to him, she felt more average than ever.

"Maybe we should start with the obvious?" she asked. "My last name. Paine. If my Dad still lives here, maybe he's listed."

Caleb smiled. "You think he'd make his number public?"

"I doubt it. But sometimes the most obvious answers are the best ones. Anyway, can't hurt to try. You've any other ideas?"

Caleb stood there, staring. Finally, he shook his head.

"Let's do it," she said.

For the millionth time, she wished she still had her cell. Instead, she looked around and spotted an Internet café across the street.

*

Caitlin had typed every variation on "Paine" she could think, and still, there were no results. She was annoyed. They had searched every possible residential and business listing in Salem. They had tried Paine and Payne and Pain and Paiyne. Nothing. Not one single person.

Caleb was right: it was a silly idea. If her father did live here, he wasn't going to make his number public. And she had a feeling, given the mysterious clues so far, that he would never make it that easy on them anyway.

Sighing, she turned to Caleb.

"You were right. A waste of time."

"*The rose and the thorn meet in Salem*," Caleb said slowly, again and again.

She could see him thinking.

She had been repeating the phrase in her mind, too, and it felt good to hear it out loud. She had been turning it over and over, but still had no idea what it meant. A rose? A thorn?

"Maybe there's a rose garden somewhere?" she said, thinking out loud. "And maybe there's some sort of clue hidden underneath it?" she said. "Or maybe it's the name of a place?" she added. "Maybe there's a bar, or an old inn, called the Rose and the Thorn?"

Caitlin turned back to the computer, and tried several variations of the search. She tried just *rose*. Then just *thorn*. Then *rose and thorn*. Businesses establishments. Parks. Gardens.

No results.

Annoyed, she finally reached over and shut the system down.

They both sat in silence for several minutes, thinking.

"Maybe we're thinking about this the wrong way," Caleb suddenly said.

She turned to him. "What do you mean?"

"Well, we've been looking for a living person," he said, "in today's world. In this century. But vampires have lived for *thousands* of years. When one vampire says to another, *come meet me*, he doesn't always mean in this century. Vampires think in centuries, not years.

"It could be that your father is not here now. But that he was. A very long time ago. It could be that we shouldn't be searching for a living person. But one who lived here at some point. And maybe even died here."

Caitlin stared at him, not really understanding.

"Died? What are you saying? My father is dead?"

"It's hard for me to explain this to you, but you need to think about this differently. Vampires live through many incarnations. Many of us have gravestones, even though we are living today. I myself, under different names, am buried in many cemeteries in many countries. Obviously I am not really dead, or buried. But at the time, the locals needed to be assured that I was. We had to stop the evidence, reassure them that I wasn't coming back to life. And a burial and a tombstone was the only thing that would put them at ease.

"The vampire race does not like to leave trails, and we do not like it when humans know that we have come back. It brings too much unwanted attention. So, sometimes, when there is no other choice, we let them bury us. And then we sneak out, quietly, in the middle of the night, and move on."

He turned and looked at her.

"It could be that your father was buried here. Maybe we shouldn't be searching above ground, but below it. We have checked the living Paines. But we have not checked the dead ones."

*

Caitlin was taken aback as they walked in the small graveyard, her mind still reeling. She had never been in a place this old before. When they had entered, a large sign had read "The Burying Point, 1637." She marveled at the fact that people had been coming here for almost 400 years.

More than that, she marveled that there were a few tourists wandering the cemetery right now. She had assumed they would have been the only ones here. But after all, this was Salem. And this cemetery was an attraction. People seemed to come here and treat it as a museum. In fact, she noticed that there was an actual museum adjacent to the burial plots. It didn't feel right to her. She felt that this place should have been more sacred.

The cemetery was small and intimate, the size of someone's backyard. A cobblestone path twisted and turned its way throughout the place, and as she strolled, she marveled at how old the tombstones were, at their strange fonts, worn away with age. It was English, but it was so old, and so quaint, it almost read like a different language.

She carefully read the names, particularly scrutinizing the last names.

But she couldn't find a single "Paine," or any variation on the name. They had reached the end of the trail. There was nothing.

As Caitlin reached the end, Caleb beside her, she stopped and read a plaque. It described some of the horrific tortures that the witches had suffered. One of them, she read, was "pressed" to death. She was horrified.

"I can't believe what they did to them," Caitlin said. "It seems like all the witches met horrible deaths."

"They weren't witches," Caleb said gravely.

Caitlin looked over at him, hearing sadness in his voice.

"They were our kind," he said.

Caitlin's eyes opened wide. "Vampires?" she asked.

Caleb nodded, looking down at the stones.

Silence settled over them, as Caitlin pondered that.

"I don't understand," she finally said. "How were they here?"

Caleb sighed. "The Puritans. They weren't persecuted in England because of their form of Christianity. They were persecuted because they were our kind. That is why they left Europe, and why they came here. To practice freely. They were trying to escape the oppression of the old world, the European vampires. They knew that if they were to survive, they would need to found a new nation. So they came. They were the benevolent vampire race, and they didn't want to war with other vampires, or with humans. They just wanted to be left alone.

"But over time, the darker vampire races followed them here, and in increasing numbers. The early wars in the colonies weren't between humans: they were really wars between good and evil vampire races.

"And the persecution of witches in Salem was just a front for a persecution of vampires.

Wherever there is good, bad follows. A perpetual battle between light and dark. The witches who were persecuted and hung in Salem were all of the good vampire race.

"This is why it would make perfect sense for your father to be buried here. Why Salem, in general, makes perfect sense. Why your necklace makes perfect sense. It all points to the same thing: that you are the one heir. The key to finding the sword they hid, that will protect us all."

Caitlin looked around the cemetery again, her mind spinning from all the history. She didn't know what to make of it. But she did know one thing: there was no "Paine" here. It was another dead-end.

"There's nothing here," Caitlin finally said.

Caleb surveyed the graveyard one more time, and seemed clearly disappointed.

"I know," he said.

Caitlin was afraid their search was really over this time. She couldn't let it end here.

"The rose and the thorn, the rose and the thorn," she said, again and again, whispering it to herself, willing herself to find the answer.

But nothing came.

Caleb began to wander the path again, and Caitlin began to wander, too, thinking as she went.

She soon came to another large plaque, nailed to a tree. At first she read just to distract herself, but as she continued reading, she suddenly became excited.

"Caleb!" she yelled. "Hurry!"

He hurried over.

"Listen to this: 'Not all of the witches who were persecuted are buried in this graveyard. In fact, only a small portion of them are. There were over 130 other witches on the 'accused' list. Some escaped, and some are buried elsewhere. For the complete list, see the museum's records.'"

They looked at each other, both thinking the same thing, and turned and stared at the museum beside them.

*

The sun was setting, and just as they reached the museum door, it was literally being closed in their face. Caleb stepped up and put out a hand, stopping the door.

An old lady's face appeared in the crack, stern and annoyed.

"I'm sorry, folks, but we are closed for the day," she said. "Come back tomorrow if you like."

"Forgive us," Caleb said gracefully, "but we need just a few minutes. I'm afraid we cannot return tomorrow."

"It's five after five," she snapped. "We close at five. Every day. No exceptions. Those are the rules. I can't keep this place open for everyone who comes in late. Like I said, if you want to come back, come back tomorrow. Good night."

She began to close the door again, but Caleb held it open with his hand. She stuck her head back out, twice as annoyed.

"Listen, do you want me to call the cops –"

Suddenly, she froze mid-sentence, as her eyes locked with Caleb's. She just stared at him, for several seconds, and Caitlin saw her expression change. It softened. Then, amazingly, she broke into a smile.

"Well, hello folks," she said, completely cheery. "So happy to see you here. Please come in," she said, opening the door widely and stepping back with a smile.

Caitlin looked at Caleb, shocked. *What had he just done?*

Whatever it was, she wanted to learn it herself.

Don't worry, you will.

Caitlin looked at Caleb and was twice as shocked to realize that he had just sent her a thought, and that she had heard it.

*

They had the museum to themselves as they walked down its narrow, dimly-lit hallways. Pictures, plaques and paraphernalia lined the walls, all of witches, judges, and hangings. It was a solemn place.

As they continued, they came to a large display. Caitlin began to read, and was so taken by it, she decided to read it aloud to Caleb.

"Listen to this," she said. "'In Salem, in 1692, a large group of teenage girls suddenly fell ill. Most of them lapsed into a fit of hysteria, and screamed out that they had been attacked by witches. Many of these girls went so far as to name the witches who were afflicting them.

"Because their illnesses were so mysterious, and because many of these girls died suddenly and there was no other explanation for it, the townspeople fell into a frenzy. They hunted down the people accused of witchcraft.

"It is worth noting that, to this day, no one has ever been able to determine the nature of the illness that struck these girls, or why they were all struck by such hysteria."

"It's because they were coming of age," Caleb said softly.

Caitlin looked at him.

"Just like you," he said. "They were our kind, and the feeding pangs were beginning to overtake them. They were not sick. They were hysterical. They were overwhelmed by what they were becoming, and unsure how to handle it."

Caitlin thought hard. Teenage girls. 1692. Salem. Coming-of-age. Going through the same exact thing that she was going through now.

It was overwhelming. She felt such a connection to history; she no longer felt alone with what she was going through. Yet she was terrified at the same time. It validated her. But she didn't want validation. She wanted someone to tell her that this was all not true, all just a fantastical nightmare, and that everything would be back to normal soon. But the more she learned, the more she was overcome by a feeling of dread. The more she realized that things would never go back to normal for her.

"Here it is," Caleb said, from the other side of the room.

Caitlin hurried over.

"The list. The 133 accused."

They both slowly looked over the long list of people, handwritten in an antique scrawl. It was hard to decipher the handwriting, and it was slow-going.

But at some point, close to the end of the list, Caitlin suddenly froze. She reached out with her finger and pointed at the glass.

There was her last name. Paine. Spelled exactly like hers. On the list of the "Accused."

"Elizabeth Paine. Accused of witchcraft. 1692."

Elizabeth? A woman?

"I knew it," Caleb said. "I knew there was a connection."

"But…" Caitlin began, so confused, "…*Elizabeth*. That's a woman. I thought we were looking for my Dad?"

"It is not so simple. Remember, we are dealing with generations. It could be that we are looking for Elizabeth. Or it could be that we are looking for her father. Or husband. We don't know where your ancestry begins or ends. But we do know there is a connection."

"Look at this!" Caitlin said excitedly, hurrying a few feet away, to a different exhibit.

They both stood and stared. It was incredible. An entire exhibit devoted to Elizabeth Paine.

Caitlin read aloud: "Elizabeth Paine was unique among those on the Accused list. She would go on to great notoriety, immortalized in *The Scarlet Letter*. It is widely accepted that its famous heroine, Hester Prynne, was actually based on the life of Elizabeth Paine. She was the centerpiece of the greatest work of a longtime Salem resident, Nathaniel Hawthorne."

Caitlin suddenly looked at Caleb, her eyes open wide in excitement.

"That's it," she said, breathlessly. She was hardly able to contain her excitement.

"What?" he asked. He still didn't see it.

"Don't you see?" she said. "The riddle. It's a play on words. Hawthorne. *The rose and the thorn.* The thorn is Haw*thorne*. And the rose is scarlet. As in, *The Scarlet Letter*. In other words, it's about Hawthorne. And Paine."

At that moment, the old woman entered the room again, seemingly coming back to her senses. She looked at them both, and said, "I'm sorry, but I really do need to close up now —"

Caitlin hurried over to her, grabbing her arm. "Where did Hawthorne live?"

"Excuse me?"

"Nathaniel Hawthorne," she said excitedly. "It says he once lived in Salem."

"Young lady, we know exactly where he lived. Thanks to our historic trust, his house was preserved. In fact, it still stands here, to this day. Perfectly intact."

Caitlin and Caleb looked at each other.

They both knew where they had to go to next.

TEN

The sun was setting as Caitlin and Caleb approached Hawthorne's house. The simple, red house was set back about 50 feet from the sidewalk, with its walkway and bushes, looked like any other small, suburban house. With its dark red paint and shutters, it had an antique simplicity about it. It was modest.

Still, one could tell it was different. It exuded history.

They both stood there, looking at it, and a silence fell over them.

"I thought it would be bigger," Caitlin said.

Caleb stood there, furrowing his brows.

"What's wrong?"

"I remember this house," Caleb said. "I'm not sure from when. But I seem to remember it being somewhere else."

Caitlin looked at him, at his perfectly sculpted features, and marveled at how much he remembered. She wondered what it was like to remember so much. Hundreds of years— thousands. He was carrying around things, experiences, that she could never even dream of. She wondered if it was a blessing or a curse, and she wondered if she would even want that for herself.

She took a few steps forward, to the iron fence enclosing the property, and as she tried the latch, she was surprised to find it locked. She looked at the sign: *9AM to 5PM Weekdays*.

She checked her watch: 5:30. Closed.

"Now what?" she asked.

Caleb looked furtively around, and she did, too. There was no one in sight on the suburban street. She got what he was thinking. He looked at her, and she nodded.

He reached over the metal latch and in one smooth motion, ripped it off its hinges. He looked around again, saw no one coming, and opened the fence and motioned for her to hurry through. He closed the gate behind them as best he could, gently laid the metal latch down in the grass, then hurried after her down the walkway.

Caitlin reached the front door, and turned the knob. Locked.

Caleb stepped up, reached for the knob, and prepared to break it.

"Wait," Caitlin said.

Caleb stopped.

"Can I try this one?" she asked, and broke into a mischievous smile.

She wanted to see if she had that kind of strength. She felt it, coursing through her veins, but didn't know its limitations, or when or where it would come.

He smiled at her and stepped aside. "Be my guest."

She tried the knob, and it didn't give. She tried harder, and still nothing. She felt frustrated, and embarrassed.

She was about to let it go, when Caleb said, "Concentrate. You're turning it like a human. Go deeper. Turn it from a different place in yourself. Let your body turn it for you."

She closed her eyes and breathed deeply. She placed her hand gently on the knob and tried to focus, following his instructions.

She turned it again, and this time was surprised to hear a snapping noise. She looked up and saw that she had broken the knob. The door was ajar.

She looked over at Caleb, and he smiled back.

"Very good," he said and gestured for her to enter. "Ladies first."

The house was cozy, with low ceilings and six over six windowpanes. The outside light was fading fast, and they hadn't much time to search, unless they wanted to start turning on lights. They walked quickly through, floorboards creaking, trying to take it all in as fast as they could.

"What are we looking for exactly?" she asked.

"Your guess is as good as mine," he said. "But I agree that we're in the right place."

At the end of the hall, there was a large exhibit devoted to Hawthorne's life. She stopped and read aloud: "Nathaniel Hawthorne was more than just another author who wrote about Salem. He lived in Salem. Most of his stories are set in Salem. Most of the buildings he described in Salem are integral to his stories, and many of them still stand here today.

"More importantly, Hawthorne had a direct personal connection to some of the events and characters in his work. His most famous work, for example, *The Scarlet Letter*, tells the story of a woman, Hester Prynne, who is imprisoned and scorned by her peers for her adulterous behavior. Hawthorne had a more direct connection to these events than one would think. His real grandfather, John Hawthorne, was one of the principal judges in the Salem witch trials. John Hawthorne was responsible for accusing, judging, and putting the witches to death. It was a heavy Salem ancestry that Hawthorne had to bear."

Caitlin and Caleb started at each other, each becoming more intrigued. Clearly, there was a strong connection here, and they both felt that they were onto something. But they still didn't quite know what. There was still a missing link.

They continued through the house, examining various objects, searching for something, anything. But as they finished searching the first floor, they came up empty.

They both stopped before a narrow, wooden staircase. It was blocked by a velvet rope, on which hung a sign: "Private: upstairs for staff only."

Caleb gave Caitlin a look.

"We've come this far," he said.

He reached over and unclasped the rope.

Excited, she went first, her footsteps echoing on the hard, wooden staircase. The house creaked and groaned as they went, as if protesting its new visitors.

The second floor of the house had even lower ceilings, barely high enough for Caleb to stand in. It was now almost dark, and there was just enough light to see by. They stood in a beautiful and cozy room, with wide plank wooden floorboards, six over six windowpanes, and tastefully decorated with period furniture. At its center was a brick fireplace with black stain around its edges, clearly worn from years of use.

Greeting them at the top of the staircase was yet another exhibit, this one devoted to Elizabeth Paine.

Caitlin read aloud: "Hester Prynn, Hawthorne's most famous character, the woman at the center of *The Scarlet Letter*, the woman who was persecuted for refusing to reveal the true identity of her child's father, was, many scholars say, based on a real life Salem resident: Elizabeth Paine. No scholar has ever been able to identify the lineage of Elizabeth's child, as she refused to reveal to any of the townsfolk who the father really was. Legend has it that he was a mysterious man, come over on a ship from Europe, and that their romance was a forbidden one.

"Elizabeth was banished from Salem and forced to live in a small cottage, by herself and with her child, in the woods, on the outskirts of town. The exact location of her cottage has never been found."

Caitlin looked to Caleb. She was speechless.

"A forbidden romance?" she asked. "As in…."

Caleb nodded. "Yes. It was between a vampire and human. His story is not really about adultery. It is all masked, hidden. It's an allegory. It's really about us. Our kind. More specifically: it's about you. Their child. The half breed."

Caitlin felt the world spinning beneath her. The ramifications were overwhelming.

She also couldn't help feeling that the story was repeating itself, that, generations later, she was playing out the same pattern. A forbidden romance. Two races. Her and Caleb. Repeating history once again, following in the footsteps of her ancestors. It made her wonder if lifetime after lifetime just repeated itself, endlessly.

They slowly surveyed the room. It was hard to see in the fading light, and she still didn't know exactly what she was looking for. But now, she definitely, without a doubt, knew that they were looking in the right place.

So, apparently, did Caleb. He walked around the room curiously, inspecting everything. They both felt sure that whatever it was they needed would be in this room. Maybe even the sword itself?

But the room was sparsely furnished, and after she inspected, she didn't see where anything could be hiding.

"Here," Caleb finally said.

Caitlin hurried over to him. He stood beside an antique hutch.

He felt the side of it with his hand. "Look at this," he said.

He took her hand, and guided it along the side, and she felt it. It had a small, metal indent. In the shape of a cross.

"What is it?" she asked.

"I don't know," he answered, "but I do know one thing: it doesn't belong on this piece of furniture. And I suspect something else: this unusual shape, the curved lines: I would bet anything that is the exact shape of your cross."

She looked at him blankly, not comprehending what he was talking about. Then she suddenly realized and reached down. Her necklace.

"I think it's a key," he said.

She took it off quickly, and together, her hand on his, they inserted it gently into the indent. She was ecstatic to see that it fit perfectly. It entered with a soft click, and as they gently turned it to the right, a narrow, vertical compartment opened.

Heart pounding, Caitlin reached inside and gently extracted a frail scroll, yellowing, brittle. It was tied with an ancient piece of string, all but crumbling.

She handed it to Caleb, and the two of them unrolled the scroll together.

It was a map. Handwritten, hundreds of years old.

At the top of the map, in a handwritten scrawl, it read: Elizabeth's cottage.

He looked up at her.

"Her cottage," he said, breathlessly. "It's a map to where she lived."

She stared at it, in awe.

"Whoever stored it here wanted you to be the one to find it. Your necklace was the key. And it's never been opened until now. He wanted you to find this map, to find her cottage. Wherever it is, there will be something in it for you."

It was meant for *her*. For Caitlin, and Caitlin alone. The thought of it overwhelmed her. Made her feel, for the first time in her life, wanted. Loved. Important. That she had a connection to something greater than herself, something hundreds of years old. That she was the center of this entire puzzle. She could hardly contain her emotions.

Then, suddenly, it happened. A horrible pain gripped her stomach. It knocked the wind out of her, and she keeled over, gasping for breath.

"Are you all right?" Caleb asked, as she felt his hand on her shoulder.

The feeding pangs. They were back. They hurt so badly this time, she could barely breathe.

Another pang suddenly struck, and this one hurt so much, she stood up with a jolt. She heard herself growl, a horrible, unearthly sound, and she saw herself running across the room, trying to get the pain out of her body. She ran right into a big exhibit, knocking it over, and heard it shatter.

But she couldn't control herself. She was spinning, out of control, and she was going to destroy everything in this room.

Caleb appeared beside her, grabbing her firmly.

"Caitlin," he said firmly, "Caitlin, listen to me!"

He grabbed her by the shoulders with all his might, but he was barely able to contain her.

"You are going to be all right. It's just the feeding pangs. Do you hear me? It's going to be all right. You just need to feed. We need to get you out of here," he enunciated slowly. "Now!"

Caitlin looked up, and in her haze, barely saw him. On one level, she heard him, but on the other, it hurt too badly. It was overwhelming her. A desire to feed. To destroy. To get her fill. Now.

Caleb must've seen whatever it was overcoming her, because, before she could react, he quickly and firmly took her arm, and let her down the staircase, and out the house.

It was nearly dark as they hurried out the front door of Hawthorne's house and down the walkway. They were moving so fast, they didn't even look up, and didn't even realize that they were walking right into a huge trap.

"Freeze!" yelled a voice.

Standing before them, guns drawn, stood several Salem policemen.

"Hands in the air! Slowly!"

Caitlin was still in a haze. The pangs struck her sharply, and she couldn't resist the waves of rage, of violence, that were overcoming her. It was hard to focus, to hear exactly what they were saying. She saw the police, but she had no fear of them. On the contrary, she wanted to pounce.

Through her haze, she felt Caleb's strong grip, clasping her shoulders, and it was the only thing that kept her in check.

"I said, hands in the air!" screamed a cop, as the two other officers came in closer.

"Calm, Caitlin, calm," Caleb whispered, as he slowly, still clutching the scroll, raised his arms high in the air, and prodded her to follow. "They can't harm us."

Caitlin, though, felt anything but calm. She saw the police, saw them pointing a gun at Caleb, and felt a red hot rage. A pang struck again, and she could no longer control herself as she zoomed in on a policemen, on his throat, the blood coursing through it. She needed it.

Caitlin pounced. She leapt right for the center policemen, and before he could react, she was on him, clutching him, her head back, teeth protracted, sinking right for his neck.

And then: a gunshot.

ELEVEN

The clock struck midnight as Kyle descended down the marble staircase, flanked by two dozen of his minions. It had been a long night, and it had done gone far better than he had ever dreamed. Still, he dreaded greeting his master, Rexius, their coven leader. They had been together for thousands of years, and he knew that Rexius was not a man who suffered fools lightly. He had zero tolerance for mistakes, and Kyle had felt nervous ever since he'd let that girl, Caitlin, escape his grasp. Rexius always punished even the smallest transgression, and Kyle had been bracing himself, wondering when his punishment would come. He knew that Rexius was just biding his time, that he would never forget.

Still, Kyle's work had gone so spectacularly tonight, in every corner of the city, that Kyle couldn't imagine how his master could remain upset with him. It should more than make up for such a small mistake. After all, they were in the midst of a historic moment in time, and Kyle was the general of this war. How could his master possibly punish him now?

Indeed, the more Kyle thought about it, the more he looked forward to this meeting. He looked forward to reporting the strength of the plague, how fast it was spreading, how well he and his men had distributed it. He looked forward to Rexius' approval, to his shared excitement that the war they had been waiting for for thousands of years was finally here.

As Kyle continued deep underground, deep under City Hall, down another marble corridor, and through a huge set of medieval doors, he felt intoxicated. He had been waiting for this day for years. He loved the feeling of the huge entourage behind him, of the war that was about to come. He hadn't felt this giddy since he'd witnessed the beheadings of the French Revolution.

As Kyle entered his master's chamber and walked through the set of double doors, several senior vampires stepped up behind him and blocked his entourage from following. They closed the door with a bang, leaving Kyle alone in the room. Kyle wasn't thrilled about this. But then again, when dealing with Rexius, you never had a choice. And you never knew what he would do next.

It was a huge, cavernous room, and as Kyle looked about, he was surprised to see hundreds of vampires lined up silently along the wall. Their numbers had already grown dramatically, and there were many vampires Kyle didn't recognize.

These vampires stood silently, at attention, along the sides of the room, practically out of sight. Only the leader dominated the room. Rexius. He sat in the center, as always, on his huge marble throne, and stared down at Kyle. That was the way the leader always wanted it.

Kyle step forward and bowed his head.

"My master," Kyle said.

A heavy silence blanketed the room.

Kyle looked up.

"You will be pleased to know, my master, that our work has gone beautifully. The plague has spread through every corner of the city. Within days, the humans will all be at their knees."

Several seconds of uncomfortable silence followed, as Kyle could feel his master glaring down at him. Those icy blue eyes—they always made his skin crawl.

Kyle finally looked down, bowing his head again. He couldn't stand looking up anymore.

"You have done well, Kyle," the leader said slowly, in a dark, deliberate, gravelly voice. "Other covens are already reporting in. Our numbers grow stronger as we speak."

"The war is going to be magnificent, master," Kyle said. "I am honored to lead it for you."

Several more seconds of silence followed.

"Indeed," Rexius finally said, "this war will be magnificent. Within days, New York will be ours, and within weeks, the human race will be enslaved."

Rexius broke into a smile, licking his lips ever so slightly. Kyle dreaded when he did that. A smile from Rexius only meant one thing: bad news.

"I am sorry to report," Rexius continued, "that you won't be here to share it with us."

Kyle felt a pain his chest, and looked up in fear. He didn't know what to say. Where would he be? Was he assigning him elsewhere?

"Not here?" Kyle asked, dumfounded. He could hear his own voice cracking, and felt ashamed. "My master, I am afraid I do not understand. I have already executed everything perfectly."

"I know you have. That is the only reason you are still breathing right now," he said.

Kyle swallowed hard.

"There remain your past mistakes to be accounted for. I never forget, Kyle."

Kyle swallowed again, and he felt his throat go dry. This was what he had been dreading.

"You let that half-breed escape. She may lead someone else to the sword. If so, our war will be compromised." He learned forward, so Kyle could see the full effect of his icy blue eyes. "*Severely* compromised."

Kyle knew better than to try to defend himself. That would only make matters worse. So instead, he just knelt there, waiting, trembling in rage, in fear. He had been tricked. He had waged their war perfectly, and now he would be punished for it.

Several seconds of silence followed, as Kyle wondered what his future would hold.

"Kyle of the Blacktide Coven, you have failed in your duties, and broken our holy covenant. I hereby sentence you to partial emergence in Ioric Acid, followed by banishment from our coven forever. You are no longer among us. You will live, but it will be a lonely life, and we will no longer recognize your name. You are an outcast. Forever."

Kyle's eyes opened wide in fear and astonishment, as dozens of minions suddenly appeared and grabbed his arms, dragging him away. It was too extreme, this punishment. It was unfair.

"But my master, you can't do this. I have been your greatest soldier—for centuries!"

Kyle struggled, as more and more arms grabbed him, dragging him backwards.

"I can find her!" he screamed, while being dragged. "I can bring her back! I and I alone! I know how to find her. You must give me this chance!"

"You have had too many chances already," the leader said, with an icy smile. "I will find her myself. I have other soldiers in my army."

It was the final thing Kyle heard as he was dragged out of the chamber, out through the double doors.

"My master!" Kyle started to scream, but before he could finish, the doors had slammed in his face.

Kyle felt the arms on him, all over him, and before he knew it, he was on his back, flat on a slab of stone.

More and more vampires pinned him down, hovering over him. It was a frenzy of vengeance. He thought of his thousands of years, of all the vendettas he had accumulated. He had stepped on a lot of toes to get where he was. Now it was time for payback.

One of them, sneering down at him, stepped forward with a bucket, and Kyle could smell the awful stench of the Ioric Acid before he even saw it.

"NO!" Kyle screamed. He had seen others suffer from it, and he could already guess the horrible pain that awaited.

As he looked up, the last thing he saw was the bucket tilting, then the liquid beginning to pour, right for his face.

And then the halls filled with the sound of his shrieking.

TWELVE

As Caitlin flew with Caleb in the cold air, gripping him tightly, her hunger pangs started to dissipate, and her head finally started to clear. She looked down and saw the blood all over Caleb, all over both of them, and tried to remember what had happened.

She remembered leaving Hawthorne's house. Then the police, then losing control. Then there was a gunshot. Yes, now she remembered. As she had aimed her teeth for the officer's neck, she had suddenly been pulled off him by Caleb. With lightning speed, he had yanked her off, had spared her from attacking another human.

But he had suffered for it. That cop had fired, and had hit Caleb in the arm. His blood had been all over both of them, but it never seemed to slow him down. Instead, he somehow managed to knock out all three policemen before they could react, to pick her up in the same motion, and to take off into the air. She marveled at his sense of control, in every situation. He had managed to get them out of there without seriously hurting anyone but himself. She felt embarrassed that she was not as evolved, not as in control, as he, and felt badly that she had once again put him in harm's way.

It was dark as Caitlin and Caleb flew over the woods, on the outskirts of Salem. As they flew in the cold, night air, she slowly felt herself calming. Caleb's strong, icy grip held her in the air, and she felt the tension in her body starting to leave. The hunger faded. So did her rage.

By the time they landed in the woods, she felt back to normal. With her head clear, the events of the past hour seem like a wild and crazy blur, and she couldn't understand why she'd reacted the way she had. Why had she been so filled with rage, so quickly? Why couldn't she control herself?

Of course, she knew the answer was not intellectual: when the pangs struck her, she was simply out of control. A different person, at the mercy of her animal instincts. Thank God for Caleb. She wouldn't have wanted that policeman's blood on her head. She was so grateful that he had rescued her before she could do anything rash.

As she saw the blood dripping down his arm, she again felt guilty. He was shot because of her.

She reached over and put her hand on his arm.

He looked down.

"I'm so sorry," she said. "Are you going to be okay?"

"It will be fine," he said. "Vampires are not like humans: our skin heals quickly. Within a few hours, it will be completely healed. It was just a regular bullet. If it had been silver, then that would have been very different. But it wasn't. So please don't worry," he said gently.

As she looked at his arm, she saw that it was already healing fast. It was amazing. It hardly looked like more than a large black and blue mark. It was as if it were healing before her eyes.

She wondered if she had a similar power. Then again, being only a half-breed, she probably didn't. Like most vampire powers, it was probably reserved only for true, full-bred vampires. A part of her wished that she was one. Immortality. Superpower. Immunity to most weapons. She had some of those traits, but clearly not all. She was stuck between two worlds, and she didn't know which one to choose.

Not that she was being given much of a choice anyway. The only way to become a true, full vampire would be to be turned by one. And Caleb wasn't offering. That was forbidden. And even if it wasn't, she had a feeling he wouldn't offer anyway. He seemed to be oppressed by being immortal, and he seemed to envy her her mortality. She didn't get the feeling that he'd want her to be what he was. For her own sake.

"Do you still have it?" he asked.

She looked over, not understanding.

"The map," he added.

Of course. The reason why they had landed here.

She reached into her pocket, and was relieved to discover it was still there. Thank God for zippered pockets.

She handed it to him.

He unrolled it and stared.

"We are not far," he said, lowering it and looking at the woods before them. "The cottage should be close."

Caitlin looked all around her, squinting in the darkness. All she saw were trees.

"I don't see anything," she said.

"It's an old map," he said. "It was drawn by hand, and is very rough. I'm sure it is not exact. But the markings indicate this area."

Caleb looked around again, and she did, too. But neither of them saw anything.

"This cottage," Caitlin said, "was here hundreds of years ago. Isn't it possible that it's been destroyed?"

Caleb scrutinized the woods. He headed in a particular direction, and she walked with him, leaves rustling.

"Yes," he said, "that is possible. Especially if it was built of wood. Then it is most likely. But I am hoping it was built of stone. Most vampire cottages were. Then it could still stand. Or at least a portion of it."

"But even if so, don't you think that by now it would have been discovered, or vandalized?" she asked.

"Possibly. Unless…"

She waited. "Unless?"

"Unless it has become overgrown. There is a tradition among vampires, a way to pass a clue on to generations. We build a stone cottage, and then plant wisteria, thorns, layers of thickets closely around it. If left alone, it grows wildly, quickly, so thick and deep, that over time, if it were a remote place, it stays untouched and is virtually impossible for a layperson to see. This way, centuries later, the initiated could still find it."

He looked around.

"The one advantage we have here is that this forest is remote. That gives me hope."

"Assuming that was a real map," Caitlin said, playing devil's advocate. "Maybe it was planted by someone. Maybe it's a false lead."

Caleb looked at her and smiled.

"You have a very sophisticated mind," he said. "Perhaps you are over thinking this. Yes, that is possible. But I doubt it. That scroll was genuine."

He took her hand as they walked deeper into the forest, the only sound, that of leaves rustling. She could feel the cold sinking into her bones.

Caleb suddenly removed his large, leather coat and draped it around her shoulders. As always, she was amazed at how he could read her mind, and touched by his generosity.

"No," she said, "I can't take your – "

"Please," he responded. "I am not cold."

As he draped his coat around her shoulders, Caitlin loved the feel of it. It was surprisingly heavy, and the inside was still warm from his body heat. She loved the smell of the leather. It felt so worn in, so comfortable, as if he had been wearing it for hundreds of years. It was way too big for her, but somehow it fit perfectly. Wearing it, she felt as if she were his. As if they were boyfriend and girlfriend. She loved the feeling.

Caleb looked down, checked the scroll, and looked back up at the woods. Still nothing.

Caitlin turned herself, in every direction, and squinted into the darkness with all she had.

As her eyes adjusted, she thought she spotted something.

"Caleb," she said.

He turned, and she raised a finger.

"See that? On the horizon. It looks like a thicket of branches. Do you think?"

He looked at it and squinted. Finally, he took her hand, and led her towards it. "Nothing to lose," he said.

As they walked towards it, leaves rustling, getting closer, Caitlin felt encouraged. It was a huge, impenetrable thicket of tangled branches and thorns. It almost looked like a wall. They circled it, and it must've been 100 feet deep in every direction. It was impenetrable. If anything fit his description, this was it. No one could get anywhere near this thing, unless they had a thick machete, and were willing to spend days chopping. Whatever was at its center—if anything—would likely be untouched.

But then again, maybe this was just a huge thicket of branches and thorns, and all that they would find for their trouble was more thorns.

Caleb nodded slowly. "Yes," he said. "This could be it."

He studied it for a while, the finally said, "Stand back."

Caitlin took several steps back, wondering what he would do.

Caleb pulled his sleeves down, over his hands, shielding them, then reached in, and with his incredible strength, tore at the thicket of branches. It was incredible, like watching a chainsaw attack the pile.

Within seconds, he had cleared a path, just wide enough for one person to walk through.

He was already lost deep in the thicket, when she heard his voice call out: "Here!"

Caitlin walked through the narrow pathway, through the wall of branches, a good 30 feet deep, and finally caught up to him.

She saw, over his shoulder, a small, stone wall.

"You found it," he said, and broke into a grin.

He cleared some more branches, and revealed a small, arched entryway to the tiny stone cottage. He entered, taking her hand, and she followed close behind.

It was dark and musty, and they both took a few halting steps in, before Caleb suddenly stopped. They heard something rolling beneath their feet, and Caleb reached down. He held something up.

"What is it?" she asked.

He held it high, but she couldn't really see in the darkness. Finally, he said, "Old candles. I think they're intact. Hold this."

Caitlin took it and rubbed his hands together with lightning speed. She had never seen anything like it. Within seconds, his hands were moving so fast that she could feel the heat coming off of them. He then put his hands over the tip of the candle, and held them there. After a second, he pulled back, and as he did, to Caitlin's shock, the candle was aflame. She looked up at him in awe. She wished she could do that, too.

"You have to teach me that one," she said, smiling.

In the candle light, she could see him smile. She lowered the candle to the floor and revealed several more candles, all spread out. So that was the rolling noise they'd heard. He picked one up and pulled back its wick, and she reached over and lit it. Now they each had a burning candle. And it was enough to light up the place.

The cottage was tiny, just tall enough for her to stand in, and low enough for Caleb to have to crouch. Its one room wasn't large, maybe ten by ten feet. Its walls were stone, and while they weren't perfectly aligned, there didn't seem any obvious places to hide anything in. Against the far wall was a small fireplace, filled with branches which must have gotten in through its small chimney over the centuries.

She looked down and saw that the floorboards were made of wood. Remarkably, they were still intact. But that made sense. There were no windows in the cottage, and aside from the chimney and the doorway, no way for any of the elements to get in. And given how thickly overgrown the branches were, no elements had gotten near this cottage for hundreds of years.

But otherwise, there was really not much to see, and not any obvious places to hide anything. It was completely bare. Unfortunately, it seemed like another dead end.

At least it was dry, and sheltered, and cozy. If nothing else, they could spend the night here. Maybe warm up, rest a bit.

"Think you can get the fireplace to work?" she asked.

He examined it. "I don't see why not."

He handed her the candle, went over to it, and quickly extracted all the debris and branches. Caitlin sneezed at the dust.

He reached up into the chimney and extracted more branches, and gathered them up and carried them out of the cottage.

Caitlin could hear climbing on the roof, and then heard him extracting more branches from the chimney. She suddenly felt a small draft of air, and realized he had cleared it. Seconds later, he appeared back inside, carrying a small stack of dry, burnable wood. She marveled at how fast he did everything. The speed of the vampire race. It was incredible. It made her feel so sluggish in comparison.

He placed the wood in the fireplace, took the candle from her, and lit it in several places. Within a few minutes, they had a roaring fire in the cozy little cottage. She was grateful for the heat.

She crammed their candles into the stone walls, up high, and between that and the fire, the room was now quite bright and warm. With her hands now free, she got close to the fire and leaned back against the stone wall. She rubbed her hands before it, and was starting to feel better.

Caleb followed suit, sitting on the opposite side of the fire, his back against the wall. They faced each other across the small room, their feet almost touching.

Caleb examined the room, looking at the floor, scanning the walls, then the ceiling. He looked intently at the bricks in the fireplace, scrutinizing every possible detail. Caitlin found herself looking, too. They both had the same thing on their minds: what could be hiding here? And where?

"This is definitely the place," Caleb said. "This is where Elizabeth lived. The question is: why did the map send us here? I don't see anything," he said, finally, admitting defeat.

"Neither do I," Caitlin had to admit.

A comfortable silence fell over them. After the whirlwind events of the day, she was exhausted. She was just happy that they had shelter for the night, and too tired to think of anything else. She loved the feeling of his coat around her shoulders. She felt the shape of her journal, still inside her jean pocket, and felt like taking it out and writing. But she was too tired.

She looked across the room, and studied Caleb. She marveled at how he was so impervious to the cold, to being tired, to seemingly even being hungry. In fact, if anything, he seemed to gain energy at night. He still looked in perfect condition, despite all they'd been through. Despite being shot. She looked at his arm, and saw that it was already entirely healed.

As he stared into the fire, lost in thought, his eyes glowed an intense brown, and she felt overwhelmed with the need to know more about him.

"Tell me about you," Caitlin said. "Please."

"What do you want to know?" he asked, still looking into the fire.

"Everything," she said. "The things you have seen…I can't even comprehend," she said. "What do you remember most?"

A long silence blanketed the room as Caleb sat there, brows furrowed.

"It's hard to say," he began softly. "In the beginning, in the first lifetimes, I was just overwhelmed with the thrill of being alive, century after century. I had lived when all others I cared for had died. At first, you begin to lose friends and family, and anyone you'd ever loved. That is what hurts the most. That is the hardest time. You begin to feel very, very alone.

"After the first hundred years, you begin to form attachments to places instead of people. To villages, cities, buildings, mountains. This is what you cling to.

"But as centuries turn into centuries, even these places disappear. Towns disappear. New towns arise. Countries get folded into other countries. Wars wipe out entire cultures you loved. Languages get lost. So you learn not to cling to places either."

He cleared his throat, concentrating.

"When places you love disappear, you cling to possessions. For hundreds of years, I collected artifacts, priceless treasure. I took great joy in that. But after hundreds of years, that, too, lost its luster. It becomes meaningless.

"Ultimately, after thousands of years, you look at life differently. You don't attach yourself to people, to places, or to possessions. You don't attach yourself to anything."

"Then what stays with you?" Caitlin finally asked. "What do you care about? There must be something."

Caleb stared, thinking.

"I suppose," he said, finally, "what stays with you, when all else falls away…are impressions."

"Impressions?"

"Impressions of certain people. Memories of times you spent together. How they affected you."

Caitlin wanted to choose her next words carefully.

"Do you mean, like…relationships? As in, like, romance?"

A silence covered the room. She could feel him choosing his words.

"There are all sorts of relationships that matter, but at the end of the day, romance probably stays with you the most," he finally said. "But there is more to it than that. In the beginning, it is about romance. But over time, the person…occupies a small part of you. I don't know how else to explain it. But after all the centuries, that is what remains."

Caitlin she was touched by his honesty. She had expected him to talk about where he was born, where he grew up. But he had done far more, as usual. His words impacted her, but she wasn't sure how. She didn't know how to respond.

"After so much time," he finally continued, "when you meet people, you immediately try to place how you knew them in other lifetimes. I find that anyone who I meet now, I have also spent significant time with them in some incarnation. They never remember, but I always do. I find myself waiting for the moment when I recognize how I've known them before. And then it comes, and it all makes sense."

Caitlin was afraid to ask the next question. She hesitated.

"So…what about us?"

Caitlin's brow furrowed, as he stared into the fire. He waited a long time before he responded.

"You're the only one I've ever met where everything is…obscured. I know, somewhere, that I have known you. But I still don't know how. Something is being held back from me, and I don't understand why. I can only assume that there is something about you—about us—that I'm not supposed to know."

Caitlin didn't know what to say. She felt overwhelmed with emotion for him, and she didn't trust herself to say anything. She knew that whatever she said would come out wrong.

She stood up and grabbed a log, and with a trembling hand, reached out to throw it on the fire. But she was so nervous, that the log slipped, landing on the floor with a thud.

Caitlin and Caleb both stopped and stared at each other. The thud of the wood: it was hollow. The floorboards. There was something beneath them.

At the same moment, they both hurried to the spot on the floor where the log landed, as Caleb smoothed it over with his hand. Centuries of dust were wiped away, revealing the bare wood. He rapped hard on it with his knuckles, and there was, again, a hollow sound.

"Stand back," he said, and she leaned back against the wall.

As she did, he pulled his arm back and punched the floorboard. There was cracking wood, as he punched a hole right through it, and reached in and tore up several floorboards.

Caitlin grabbed a candle, and put it inside the hole. There was not much space, and they could see the dirt on the ground. Caitlin moved the candle. At first, it revealed nothing. But as she moved the candle to the corner, she suddenly saw something. "There."

Caitlin reached in and slowly extracted it. She held it up, and wiped away an inch of dust.

It was a small, red satin pouch. Tied shut by a string.

She handed Caleb the candle, and began opening it. She wondered what on earth it could be. A coin? A piece of jewelry? Her heart pounded with excitement as she finally got it open. She reached in delicately, and felt something cold and metal.

She held it up and they both stared.

It was a small key.

She looked back in the pouch, to make sure there was nothing else. This was it. Just this key.

She handed it to Caleb. He too, held it up, getting closer to the fire, examining it every which way.

"Do you recognize it?" Caitlin asked.

He shook his head.

Caitlin came over, getting close to him, as they both sat by the fire and touched the key. As she turned it over, she noticed something. She licked her finger, and rubbed it alongside the metal. A final layer of dust evaporated, and there was visible a small inscription, written in a delicate script.

The Vincent House.

She looked to Caleb. "Do you know it?"

He leaned back, shook his head and sighed.

"I guess our search isn't over," he finally said.

She could hear the disappointment in his voice. He had clearly expected to find the sword here. She was sorry, and felt somehow to blame. She, too, was frustrated by all the clues. She leaned back herself, settling in for what she assumed might be a long search. At least this place had yielded a clue. At least it wasn't a dead end. Now, at least, they held a key. But to what?

Before she could finish the thought, Caitlin suddenly keeled over in pain. She was struck by a hunger pang, worse than any she'd ever had. She could barely catch her breath.

She felt the hand on her shoulder. "Caitlin?"

He didn't wait for her to respond. She felt a strong hand beneath her arm, then felt herself being picked up, and carried, as he sprinted with her out of the cottage, through the thicket of branches, and into the forest.

As the pains struck her, again and again, she felt herself being carried through the forest, and saw the trees whirling by her at super speed.

She felt the rage building inside of her. The desire to feed. To kill. Her body was changing rapidly, and as she squirmed in his arms, she didn't know how much longer she could keep it under control.

Caleb finally stopped, set her down, and stood her on her feet. He held her squarely by the shoulders, and looked directly at her.

"You must listen to me. I know it is hard to hear right now. But you must focus."

She tried as hard as she could to focus on his words, his eyes. Her world was misting over with a red haze, and the urge to kill coursed through her veins.

"It is the need to feed. You need blood. Now. We are in a forest. I can teach you. We can hunt together."

Teach you. Teach you. She tried to hold onto his words.

She felt herself being pulled, and before she knew it, they were off into the night.

THIRTEEN

Samantha woke at the crack of dawn, and looked over. There, in bed beside her, was the teenage boy. Sam. He had been so easily seduced. She almost felt bad. She knew she had violated a law in sleeping with a human, but this one was so young and fresh, she had decided to bend the rules. Why not? No one would ever know. Of course, she would never tell, and she wouldn't keep Sam alive long enough to tell anyone himself. Once every few hundred years, she had to indulge. It was the least she could allow herself.

Besides, there was something about him, something that, for a human, made him almost tolerable. In fact, if she were being honest with herself, more than tolerable. She couldn't quite put her finger on what it was, and this, more than anything, bothered her.

Agitated by her feelings, she sat up, still naked, and in one swift motion jumped to her feet and walked silently through the room. She picked up her clothes and dressed quickly, looking out the sliding glass doors. Dawn was breaking. *How ironic,* she thought. *Sleeping during the night, and waking in the morning. Just like a human.* The thought of it made her sick, but there were times one had to make exceptions.

She looked over her shoulder and saw the boy sleeping soundly. She had tired him out, that was for sure. She knew he'd never had an experience like it, and that he never would again. After all, she had 2,000 years of experience. He was certainly lucky. At least for now. He would be equally unlucky in the coming weeks, when she'd had her fill of him, and had found out all she needed to know about his father. Then, she would dispose of him. But for now, he was a fun toy. Quite fun.

He remained sound asleep, as she was so lithe, so limber on her feet. Like a cat. She could prance through the entire house and he would never hear a thing, unless she wanted him to. One of the many advantages of being a vampire.

He had been so gullible: he had really believed that this house was hers. She'd worried how she would explain the fact that there were no blankets or sheets or pillows—or anything in the house— but to her surprise, he didn't even ask. And the place has been at least partially furnished. Probably all the doings of some desperate broker, staging the house for his hypothetical showings. At least she had put it all to good use.

She felt the heat course again through her veins, and realized that she couldn't wait any longer. She needed to feed. It had been hard for her to mate with him and not finish it off, like she always did, with feeding. But she needed him alive. He was the key, and she'd had to control herself. But that didn't stop the hunger, and as she walked about the empty house, looking out at the breaking sky, the empty country road, she wondered if any unsuspecting humans might be walking down the path. Perhaps a small child, up too early. That would be perfect.

Before she could finish the thought, a shiny BMW came down the road, and turned into the driveway. There was the sound of gravel, as the car's shiny tires made their way slowly towards the house. Who on earth, she wondered, could be pulling into the driveway this time of day? Who knew she was there?

Her heart stopped momentarily, as she wondered if it could be a member of her coven. Had someone seen her mating? Had some rival vampire reported her, and had they come to punish her?

The car door opened and out came a human, poorly dressed in a cheap suit, carrying a "for-sale" sign beneath his arm. He walked towards the front door of the house.

She was so relieved, that she laughed out loud. It was just another pathetic human. And this one, a real estate broker. The worst of them all.

Of course. Now it made sense. He was probably preparing to show the house, probably had an open house scheduled, and was here bright and early to make sure everything was fine. Overzealous. And desperate.

As she watched him approach, she saw his brow furrow in confusion and then concern, as he began to notice the signs that the house was occupied. Sam's pickup truck in the driveway. A light on. He seemed utterly confused, as if racking his brain to remember if he'd left a light on, or whose car that could be. Then, as he seemed to realize that it was something more, his expression turned to annoyance.

Samantha smiled. She loved how annoyed he was, and she reveled in the fact that it was about to get much worse. She couldn't wait.

She opened the front door widely, and walked out, heading right towards him.

His look changed to one of outright outrage.

"What the hell are you doing in this house?" he yelled from across the lawn, strutting right towards her. "Do you realize that this is breaking and entering? You young kids think it's all a joke, that you can crash anywhere you want. I'm sick of it. You're not gonna get away with it this time. I've had just about enough of this!" he yelled in a rush, as he pulled out his cell, still strutting towards her.

She smiled even wider, and this really set him off.

"You think this is a joke, don't you?" he said, as he began to raise his phone to his ear, walking towards her with twice the speed.

As he reached her, he grabbed her roughly under her arm. He turned, thinking that he would drag her off.

His expression changed to one of shock, as he realized she had other plans. Before his fingers could fully dig into her skin, she had swept his arm around in one swift motion, and then twisted it back, snapping it cleanly in half.

His face contorted in pain as he began to scream. But before he could make any noise, she grabbed his head and brought it down right into her knee. There was a crack, and then nothing, as his body went limp.

Before his body hit the floor, she was already pouncing, sinking her teeth deep into his neck. Her eyes rolled back in her head as she fed, and fed. She felt ecstasy, as his blood coursed through her system.

When she finished, she picked up his lifeless body, went to his car, opened the trunk and threw his body in. Before she slammed it shut, she reached in and grabbed the car keys from his pants pocket.

She headed back towards the house, wiping the last remnants of blood from her mouth, and admired the morning sky.

This was going to be a great day.

FOURTEEN

Caitlin was running. She was back in the field, running through the knee-high grass. It was daybreak, and as she ran, the world seemed to rotate. She felt as if she were running right towards the large, glowing sun.

There, on the horizon, stood her father, his silhouette lit by the sun. His arms were opened wide, waiting to embrace her. She could not make out his features, but she did know that he was grinning, waiting to embrace her. If only she ran faster.

Caitlin ran for all she had, but no matter how fast she went, he kept getting farther.

She was not surprised. This was how the dream always went. A part of her knew this even as she dreamt it.

But this time, something happened. This time, suddenly, she gained ground. He was actually getting closer.

As she ran closer to him 50 yards, then 20, then 10, for the first time, she saw him. He was standing there, huge, so tall and proud, in all his glory, lit up by the sun. He was a beautiful man. A warrior. Somehow, he resembled Caleb.

She ran right into his arms and gave him a huge hug. He embraced her back. It felt so good to, finally, be in his arms.

"Daddy!" she cried.

"My child," he said, in a deep, beautiful, reassuring voice. "I've missed you so very much. I have been looking down on you. And I'm so proud of you," he said.

He took her by the shoulders, held her back at arm's length, and stared into her eyes.

His eyes were bright yellow, the color of the sun, and shining right at her.

She couldn't bear to look, but she couldn't bear to look away either. They radiated such warmth and love.

"Do you remember, Caitlin?" he asked. "Do you remember, when you were young? Where we used to go? The cliffs. The red cliffs."

An image flashed into her mind of huge, red cliffs, of gigantic rocks, spread all throughout the beach, into the water. A magical place. Yes, she remembered. It was coming back.

"Find me there," he said. "Continue your search. And find me there."

He started to fade, and as she reached out to grab him, he was suddenly gone.

Caitlin woke with a start.

She was flat on her back, looking up at the treetops. In the distance, she could see the passing sky passing, through the trees. A wisp of a cloud drifted by.

She had no idea where she was, but she still felt as if she were dreaming. She could hear the wind rustling through the delicate branches, leafless, and it felt as if the whole world were alive, swaying, making noise.

Despite being outdoors, she felt comfortable. She looked down and saw she was lying on the forest floor, in a pile of soft pine needles. A few feet away lay Caleb. Her heart swelled. It felt great to be sleeping so close to him. She hoped he wouldn't wake anytime soon, that she could lie like this forever. Everything in the world just felt right.

She looked back up at the sky, and tried to remember how they had got there. Tried to remember the night before.

She remembered the feeding. There had been a small family of deer, and Caleb had calmed her, had taught her how to wait. He had taught her how to control it. She had remembered feeling clarity.

Once she'd charged after them, her body had surprised her, had told her what to do, where to go. She'd found herself charging with lightning speed through the woods, then pouncing.

She remembered wrapping her arms around a deer's neck, and going for a ride. It had been fast, faster than she could have ever dreamt. But finally, she had found the vein and sunk her teeth in. And the feeling had been electrifying.

She had never felt so alive as the deer's blood coursed through her. She had felt on fire. Rejuvenated.

Slowly, her pains had faded, as did her hunger. And she'd felt stronger than she'd ever had. She'd felt as if the world were hers.

She looked over at Caleb. He had fed, too, last night. They had met afterwards, both so exhilarated, and then, so tired. They had laid back, on the forest floor, near each other, and had looked up at the swaying trees. Listening to the wind.

And then, within moments, they'd both fallen fast asleep.

Now, lying there, she inched closer to him, wanting to test out the feel of herself in his arms. She was still wearing his leather coat, and as she reached out, its sleeves just covering her hands, and ran the back of her hand along his cheek. It was so smooth. She imagined that they were together, a couple.

Caitlin suddenly heard a rustling, and she sat up straight.

Right in front of her, slowly approaching, was a pack of wolves. She had never seen a wolf before, and had no idea how to react. Oddly enough, she wasn't afraid. She was intrigued, mesmerized. In fact, as she watched them, she almost felt a strange sort of kinship.

While watching, she reached over and placed a hand on Caleb, shaking him.

He suddenly sat up beside her, alert. The two of them stared together as the pack came in close, only feet away, sniffing and circling.

"Don't be afraid," Caleb said softly. "I can feel their thoughts. They are just curious. Remain still."

Caitlin sat very still, watching as their leader came up close to her, inches from her face, putting its nose right up to her cheek.

Several tense moments followed, as Caitlin wondered what to do. Her heart was pounding, and she felt like pushing him away. But instead, she followed Caleb's direction and sat very still.

Suddenly, he turned and walked away.

As he left, the pack followed.

Except for one. A small wolf, a pup, hardly bigger than a small dog, lingered. It limped, and looked back at the pack. Then it turned and looked at Caitlin, and walked right to her.

It walked into her lap, sat down, and lowered its head. It was clear that it did not want to leave.

"The pack no longer wants her," Caleb said. "She's injured. She's a liability. And they are too hungry to be patient. They have abandoned her."

Caitlin tried to focus, tried to read the animal's thoughts as Caleb did. She couldn't read it exactly, but she did feel an energy, her feelings. She felt very alone. And scared.

Caitlin reached down, picked her up and held her in her arms. As she stroked the animal's head, it leaned back and licked her face.

She smiled.

"You have a friend," Caleb said.

"Can we take her?" she asked.

Caleb furrowed his brow.

"It would not be the best idea," he said. "Its scent...it could attract other things."

"But we can't leave her here," Caitlin pleaded, suddenly feeling very protective. "We *can't.*"

"Where we are going, there will be grave danger. It could get caught in the middle."

"Would it not be in danger here?" she asked. "It will die, left alone."

Caleb thought for a long time.

"I suppose we can take it..."

The wolf, as if understanding, ran over and jumped into Caleb's arms and licked his face.

Caleb broke into a big smile as he pet it. "Okay, okay, enough little fellow," he said.

"What shall we name her?" Caitlin asked.

Caleb thought. "I don't know," he finally said.

It suddenly came to her. The Rose and the Thorn.

"Rose," she said suddenly. "Let's call her Rose."

Caleb looked at her, then nodded in approval. "Rose," he said. "Yes, that is perfect."

As if responding to her new name, Rose ran back to Caitlin's lap, and cuddled into her chest.

"A family of wolves is a very powerful sign," Caleb said. "It means that the nature energy is with us. We are not alone in our search."

"I had a dream last night," Caitlin said, remembering. "It was unlike any I'd had before. It was so vivid. It was like… a visit. From my father."

Caleb turned and stared at her.

"In the dream, it all came back to me. An old memory. One summer, I remember, he took me away. To an island. There were these huge boulders by the ocean, and these steep cliffs, these red cliffs that glowed in the sun—"

Caleb's eyes suddenly lit up. "You dreamt of the Aquinnah Cliffs," he said. "Yes. That would make perfect sense."

"In my dream, he told me to return there. He said to…*find* him there."

"That was not a dream," Caleb said, sitting up straighter. "Vampires visit in morning dreams. Your father wants us to go to the cliffs."

"But what about the key we just found?" Caitlin asked.

"We don't know what it's for," he answered. "The Vincent House could be anywhere. It's as

143

good as a dead end. We have nowhere else to go."

Caleb stood. "We must go to the cliffs immediately."

FIFTEEN

Sam woke in the strange bedroom and looked around. He tried to remember where he was. The bed was comfortable, more comfortable than any he'd slept in in a long time, but he couldn't remember whose it was, or what he was doing here.

Then it came back to him. Samantha.

He turned and looked for her, but she was gone. Had this all really happened? Had it all just been a dream?

He sat up, rubbed his eyes, and realized he was naked, lying on a mattress with no bedding. His clothes were strewn out on the floor. He was exhausted, but in a great way. He was a changed man. *Man* was the key word. He woke up feeling like a real man for the first time in his life. He never had a night like that before, and he already guessed that he never would again. She was incredible.

Sam jumped to his feet, dressed, and walked around the empty house. He looked out the glass doors, and saw that the day was just breaking. That, too, was crazy. He hadn't seen the sun rising in he didn't know how long. In fact, it was rare for him to get up on any day before 12.

He was hungry, and thirsty, but mostly just exhausted.

"Samantha?" he called out, as he walked through the house, looking for her.

He went from room to room, but couldn't find her anywhere. He started to wonder if it had all truly just been a figment of his imagination.

He went to the living room and looked out the large picture window. There was his pickup truck, in the driveway. And there, behind it, was a shiny BMW. He wondered if it was hers. And why he hadn't seen it before. This chick was full of surprises.

But he really didn't care about any of that. He didn't even care about having a place to crash. He realized he just liked being around her. The smell of her. The sound of her voice. The way she moved. And, of course, last night. It was unbelievable.

But most of all, he'd really liked having someone to talk to. Someone who listened, who cared, who seemed to really get him. He was falling for this girl. He couldn't believe it, but he really was. And now, after all that, had she left?

He opened the front door, and there she was. Samantha. She had been opening the door at the same time.

"Hey," Sam said, trying to sound casual, but thrilled to see her. He felt his heart race just to see her again. She looked even prettier in the morning than she'd looked last night, her long red hair tussled over her face and her bright green eyes staring out at him. And so pale. He was pale, too—but she was paler than anyone he'd ever met.

"Hey," she said casually. She seemed self-conscious, as if he had surprised her, just caught her in the middle of something.

She brushed past him and walked into the house.

He turned and walked after her, puzzled. He wondered if he had done something wrong. Or maybe if he wasn't good enough. If she wanted him to go.

He started to feel self-conscious as he walked after her.

He heard the sound of running water. She was standing over the sink, washing her hands and pouring water over her face. She was probably just waking up, maybe out for a morning walk.

"You're up early," he said, smiling, as he watched her rinsing her face yet again.

She rested, taking her time, then reached over and took a towel, and wiped her face. She brushed some of the hair out of her face, and took a deep breath.

"Yeah," she said, exhaling, "morning jog. I'm an early riser."

"Without any shoes?" he asked.

Samantha looked down and realized she was barefoot. She felt her face redden. This boy was perceptive.

"It's better for the feet," she said, and quickly turned and walked into the other room.

Surprised at her abrupt departure, Sam wondered if she were avoiding him. Maybe she'd changed her mind. He'd probably screwed it up somehow. Figured. Whenever he found something great, he always screwed it up.

Sam followed her into the living room. He figured he needed to clear the air, talk to her.

As he entered, she was pulling her long, red hair out of her face, tying it in a ponytail. Her cheeks were flushed, and seemed to be getting more filled with color, right in front of him. *She must've had a really hard run*, he thought.

"Samantha," he began hesitantly, "last night was amazing."

She turned and looked at him, and her features softened a bit. She walked slowly to him, placed one hand on his cheek, and kissed him, slowly.

Sam's heart welled up. She wasn't sick of him. He hadn't screwed it up. He started to fill with optimism again. He wanted her.

But before he could embrace her, she backed away, went to the couch, and threw on her black leather coat.

"I'm antsy," she reported. "Let's get out of here." She looked at him. "Want to go for a drive?" she asked.

"A drive?" he asked, looking at his watch. "So early?"

"I hate sitting around," she said. "I want to get out of here. Let's get some fresh air. You game?" she asked, locking her green eyes right onto his.

When her eyes met his, he felt his thoughts changing. Almost as if he were under a spell. He found himself suddenly liking her plan: it made all the sense in the world. She was right. Why stick around this house? It was boring. He suddenly really wanted to get out there out of there, too, and in fact, couldn't stand to be there another second.

"Yeah, I do," he heard himself saying, "but where?"

"Email your Dad," she said. "Tell him we're coming to visit."

Sam felt his brows lift in surprise. "My Dad? You mean, like, now?"

"Why not? You guys wanted to get together. Now's as good a time as any. He's in Connecticut right? That'd be a nice drive."

Sam struggled to think. It all felt so sudden.

"Well, like, I don't know if he'd be ready on, like, such short notice—"

"Sam," she said, firmly, "he emails you a lot. He's dying to see you. Just email and ask him. And either way, let's just go. If he's not into it, at least we'll have a cool drive."

As he thought about it, he found his mind changing once again, and realized that she was entirely right. Of course. Why hadn't he thought of that? A long drive. Connecticut. E-mailing his Dad. Yes, it was perfect.

He whipped out his cell, logged onto Facebook, and started typing: *Dad. I want to come see you now. I'm actually heading out the door. A couple hours away. Please let me know your address. I hope it's not too short notice. Love, Sam.*

Sam shoved the phone into his pocket, then grabbed his keys and hurried to the front door. She was already waiting outside.

As they crossed the lawn, heading for the BMW, Sam said, "I like your ride."

She smiled as she held up the keys.

"Thanks," she said. "I've been saving a long time."

SIXTEEN

As Caitlin and Caleb stood by the railing, looking out at the ocean, the ferry to Martha's Vineyard blew its horn and began to depart. Caitlin looked down and saw the moving water, and was excited. She loved boats. She felt happy, and free. As she watched the waves rising beneath her, she realized that right now she'd probably be sitting in some stupid class, listening to a teacher drone on. She felt like an adult. Independent. The whole world was hers.

She looked over at Caleb, expecting to see him also happy, and was surprised to see him looking so nervous. She had never seen him like this.

He looked more pale than usual. She wondered if he didn't like boats, or if maybe he didn't know how to swim.

She reached over and lay a reassuring hand on his. "You okay?"

He nodded, and swallowed. He clutched the railing, and looked down at the water as if it were his enemy.

"What is it?" she asked.

He swallowed.

"Water," he said simply. He gripped the railing harder. "Our kind does not like water. Especially crossing it. Most won't even try."

Caitlin checked in with herself, and noticed that she felt fine. She wondered if it was because she were not a true vampire.

"Why?" she asked.

"Water acts as a form of psychic protection," he said. "When you cross a major body of water, you are crossing an energy field. It also strips our senses. It weakens them. It's harder for us to tell what others are thinking, harder to influence them, harder to sense things. It is like a fresh start. You lose the power and protection you had on the mainland."

Rose suddenly retreated further inside Caitlin's jacket. Caitlin could feel her trembling, and it seemed that she, too, was afraid. She reached in and rubbed her head.

She looked away and saw that there were only a few others on the large ferry. There were hardly any people on deck either; it was practically empty. They were lucky it was running at all, given the time of year. The cold March air, along with the mist off the waves, hardly made for the warmest ride.

"Want to go inside?" she asked.

He gripped the railing more tightly, looking out at the water.

"If you wouldn't mind," he said finally.

"Of course," she said, "I'm cold anyway."

As they walked between the rows of empty seats, they found two adjacent seats by a window.

As Caleb sat, Rose stuck her head out of Caitlin's jacket and made a soft whining noise.

"I think she's hungry," Caitlin said. "What does a baby wolf eat?"

Caleb smiled. "I don't know. Twizzlers?"

Caitlin smiled back. "I'm going to check out the concession stand. Want anything?"

Caleb shook his head, still looking a bit seasick.

Caitlin headed back, and scanned the rows of chips and candy. She ordered a hot dog for Rose, a Snickers bar for herself, then one for Caleb, too, in case he changed his mind.

As she finished paying, ready to head back, she suddenly stopped. A flyer, pinned to the wall, caught her eye. As she read it, she froze. She could hardly believe what it said.

She tore it off the wall and hurried back down the aisle.

She reached out and held the flyer before Caleb.

He looked at it, then did a double take. His jaw dropped open as he held it up.

It was an advertisement to come see Martha's Vineyard. And it listed the Vincent House.

SEVENTEEN

Sam sat in the passenger seat of the BMW as they raced down the interstate. He couldn't believe it. It all felt like a dream. Here he was, in the passenger seat of a new BMW, racing down the highway, leaning back, with a hot girl by his side. And it was *her* car, and *she* was driving—stick. She was hot to begin with, but this made her really hot. He felt like he was in some kind of James Bond movie. Things like this just didn't happen to him. Girls never even talked to him, and the few times he'd tried to pick them up, it hadn't gone so well.

And things just kept getting better. Not only did she have an awesome house, and a hot pair of wheels, but she, like him, just wanted to take off and go. They both had their windows down, and it was turning out to be a warm, March day. Coldplay came on the radio, and Sam reached over and turned it up. He wondered if she'd turn it back down, or change the station.

Instead, she reached over and turned it louder. He couldn't believe it.

Sam looked out the window, watching the trees raced by, and wondered what it would be like to meet his Dad. He couldn't believe it was really happening. After all those years of looking for him, he would be seeing him in just a few hours. He could hardly believe that all these years, his Dad had been so close by. Connecticut. Just a drive away.

Sam wondered what he looked like. He was probably a cool dude, tall, unshaven, with longish hair and a motorcycle. Maybe he had tattoos. Maybe even some piercings. He wondered where he lived, what kind of a house it was, what kind of property. He probably lived in an awesome house, like some kind of huge mansion, maybe something right on the water. Maybe he was a retired rock star.

He pictured them driving down a long driveway, lined with trees, and pulling up in front of the door. He could see his Dad opening the door, hurrying out, lighting up when he saw Sam. He saw his Dad embracing him, giving him a huge hug. And apologizing.

I'm so sorry, son. I tried to track you down for all these years. I just could never find you. It's going to be different now. You're going to live here.

Sam smiled at the thought of it. He could barely contain his excitement. He wondered if today would be a new beginning. Yes, the more he thought about it, maybe it would. Maybe he just wouldn't bother going back to Oakville. Maybe he'd just stay, move right in. Finally, he'd have some stability. Someone who actually cared about him, day in and day out. It was going to be awesome. This would be the first day of his new life.

He looked over and watched Samantha as she drove, her window down, her long, red hair whipped in the wind. She was so hot, so cool. He wondered why she cared about him, about his Dad, about taking him here. He guessed she was just the adventurous type, just like him. Always down for something new.

He wondered if it would be awkward to meet his Dad with her by side. But as he thought about it, he realized it could actually be really cool. It would make him look a lot cooler than he was. Here he was, showing up with a hot chick. His Dad would be impressed. Maybe nod at him in respect.

He wondered where Samantha would go after all this, after he moved in with his Dad. Would she stick around? Would she take off? Of course she would. She'd just bought that house in Oakville. She'd have to go back. Where would that leave the two of them?

Sam bit his lip, suddenly nervous, wondering how it would all play out, what he would do. If his Dad wanted him to move in, he would. But then again, he really wouldn't want to leave Samantha.

He'd deal with it when the time came. It was all just too much to think about right now. He just really wanted to enjoy the ride, enjoy the moment.

He felt the car growl, and watched Samantha shift to sixth gear, and saw the speedometer hit 110. He was thrilled. He wondered if she'd let him drive, too. He still didn't have his license, but he had a feeling she wouldn't care.

He finally summoned the courage to ask.

"Think I can drive?"

Samantha looked over, and broke into a smile. Her teeth were perfect, gleaming.

"Think you can handle it?"

EIGHTEEN

The ferry let Caleb and Caleb off at the dock in Edgartown, a small village in the southeast corner of Martha's Vineyard. As they walked down the ramp, Caitlin noticed that both Caleb and Rose seemed relieved to be on dry land. Rose peeked her head out, and kept it out, sniffing the air, and taking in the view with great curiosity.

Caitlin held the flyer up once again and stared. She couldn't believe their luck. It was an advertisement to explore "Historic Martha's Vineyard," and there, towards the end of the list of sites, it read: "The Vincent House. Built 1672."

After seeing it, they had decided to change plans, and to go to the Vincent House first, before the Aquinnah Cliffs. After all, that's what was engraved on the key, and that was a more concrete lead than the cliffs. Maybe they wouldn't even need to see the cliffs now. At least now they had a specific place to go. And of course, Caitlin still held the key in her pocket, holding it close. She slipped one hand into her pocket, feeling the worn silver, and felt reassured.

Caleb and Caleb walked down the long dock, which was practically empty. It was as if they had the island to themselves. Despite the time of year, the weather had warmed on their boat trip out. It was now unseasonably warm, at 65 degrees. Caitlin felt herself wanting to get rid of some of her layers of thick clothing.

She looked down, and felt embarrassed that she was still wearing the clothing she had picked up days ago, at that Salvation Army. She desperately wanted some more clothes. But she had no money on her. And she couldn't ask Caleb.

She looked over and saw Caleb adjusting his collar, apparently also affected by the warmth. It felt like a late spring day, hardly like March. The sun was brilliant, and shining everywhere, bouncing off the water and off of everything.

Caleb suddenly looked at her, and, as if reading her mind, said, "Why don't we get you some new clothes?" Before she could respond, he added, "Don't worry. I have a credit card with an unlimited credit line." He broke into a sheepish smile. "One of the advantages of being around for thousands of years. You amass wealth."

Caitlin marveled at how he could always read her thoughts. On the one hand, she loved it, but on the other, she worried as to how much he could read, exactly. Was he able to know her deepest thoughts and feelings? She hoped not. But she had a feeling that, even he did, he was able to control how deep he probed, and that he didn't pry.

"As long as you're sure it's not a problem," Caitlin said tentatively. "And that you'll let me pay you back one day."

He took her hand and led her on a walk down the main street of the quaint, historic village. Despite the beautiful weather, there were hardly any people out—probably, she assumed, because of the time of year. This seemed to be a seasonal place. She felt as if they had the whole town to themselves—and it was the most beautiful place she had ever been.

The village was so clean, so perfectly maintained, and was filled with small, historic houses, each more stunning than the next. It looked like a time set, like they had gone back to the early 1800s. The town was a quiet masterpiece.

The only thing ruining the illusion were the modern retail shops. She assumed that in the summertime, these were probably all opened and crowded with wealthy people, that this was probably one of those places that she could have never afforded to visit. She marveled at her luck. She was so happy to be here now, and with Caleb, and on such a beautiful day.

She closed her eyes and breathed in the spring air, and she could almost see herself living here with Caleb, back in time, in another century. A part of her wished that they could just stop running, just settle down here, live a normal life together. But she knew that was not meant to be.

"Should we find the Vincent House?" she asked.

"We will," he said. "Let's get you your clothes first."

He led Caitlin into the one shop that was open. Lily Pulitzer.

The quaint little bell rang as they opened the old door, and the saleswoman seemed thrilled to have customers. She put down her paper and hurried over, and couldn't have been more gracious.

Caitlin handed Rose to Caleb as she browsed, and the saleswoman was delighted.

"Wow, what a beautiful puppy," she said, her eyes opening wide. "Is that a husky?"

Caleb smiled. "Something like that," he said.

Ten minutes later they exited the store, Caitlin dressed in a new outfit from head to toe. She felt like a new person. She looked down at herself and nearly laughed aloud. It was so *not* her. She had gone from wearing all Salvation Army to being decked out in a series of pastels:

lime green jeans, a pink tee-shirt, a light purple, cashmere sweater, and a lime green Kiera coat. It's not like she had much of a choice: it was the only store open, and it was all that they had left this time of year in her size. The coat hugged her firmly, and had an inner pocket just big enough to hold her journal, which she transferred from her other jacket. For shoes, she'd bought gold, sequined flats. She could have been in a Lily Pulitzer catalog.

Well, if she was going to get caught up in a vampire war, at least she'd be fashionable. And probably the only vampire *not* wearing black.

She smiled as she recalled the saleswoman's surprised expression when she'd told her to just throw out all of the clothes she'd wore in. It must not have been every day that a customer said that.

A part of her kind of liked it. It was a whole new her. It certainly wasn't the wardrobe she'd had in mind in this journey with Caleb. She pictured herself wearing something all black, like him, maybe something leather, with high collars, something Gothic. But that was fine. They were new, and she was so grateful for that.

"Thank you so much, Caleb," she said, as they walked out the store. She really meant it. She'd never had any guy in her life buy her clothing, much less clothing this nice. And having been so kind and gracious about it. She really felt taken care of, and she was more appreciative than he would ever know.

He smiled and took her hand, as they strolled down the street. She felt so warm in her new clothing, perhaps too warm, but she knew it was an unusually hot day, and that it would be better to be too hot than too cold.

They had asked the saleswoman if she'd heard of The Vincent House and had been happily surprised that she not only knew where it was, but reported that it was only a block away.

As they headed in that direction, for the first time, they were not walking in a mad rush. They strolled, taking their time. In the back of their minds, they both had a feeling that once they got to this house, discovered the next clue, things would heat up again. They were both tired. Neither of them was in a rush to get rolling at a frantic pace again. And neither of them were too eager to find whatever was there. On the one hand, they did. But on the other, they both knew that once they found it—whatever it was, wherever it was—their lives would change irrevocably. And that would probably entail their parting ways.

Caitlin set Rose down and allowed her to walk beside them. She was happy to see that she was well behaved, keeping pace with them and not wandering off. She ran to a small patch of grass to relieve herself, but then ran right back.

Caitlin reached down and gave her another small piece of the hotdog, and she ate it happily.

They passed a large, historic church, walked alongside a small, white picket fence, and then turned and entered a walkway that led through immaculately kept grounds. The grass was green and vibrant, even this time of year. To one side of them was a magnificent old whaling Church, and to the other was an enormous whaling house from the mid-19th century, with a large veranda in the back. The sign read: "The Daniel Fisher House." It was the most beautiful house she'd ever seen. She could happily picture herself living there. Strolling through its backyard, with Caleb holding her hand and Rose by her side, it almost felt like they were home.

They continued down the walkway another hundred yards or so, and eventually it led to a small, historic house, set back from everything. She looked up at the plaque: *The Vincent House. 1672.*

They both stared at the structure. It wasn't anything much. A small, low-ceilinged house, it looked like the typical 1600s house, with only a few, tiny windows, and a low roof. It only looked large enough to hold a bedroom or two, and was a modest, wooden structure. Not what Caitlin had expected.

They walked to the front door, and Caleb reached out and tried the knob. Locked.

"Hello?" came a voice. "Can I help you?"

They both turned to see a woman in her 60s, immaculately dressed and wearing a stern expression, approaching them in an official, businesslike manner.

Caleb turned to Caitlin. "This time it's your turn," he said. "I want you to use your mind control. You can do it. Vampires have it over humans. Yours is not yet developed, and may not be as strong, but you definitely have some power. Practice on this woman. Influence her. Stay calm, and allow her thoughts to become your thoughts. Allow your thoughts to become hers. Suggest to her what she must do. In her own voice. Your mind can do it all. Just let it."

The woman, getting closer, called out again, "The house is closed for the season, like the sign says," she said, very proper. "I'm afraid you'll have to come back in-season. It's under restoration, and there are no tours before then." She looked down at Rose. "And we *certainly* don't allow dogs."

The woman, only feet away, hands on her hips, had a very stern presence, like that of a strict schoolteacher.

Rose looked up and growled back.

Caleb looked at Caitlin.

Caitlin looked at the woman, nervous. She had never tried this before, and wasn't sure if she could do it.

OK, Caitlin thought, *here it goes*.

166

She stared at the woman, trying to get a fix on her thoughts. She felt a lot of firmness, a lot of strictness. A person not easily controlled. She felt anger, annoyance, an insistence on the rules. On order. She allowed it all in.

Then, Caitlin tried to send her an outgoing thought. She tried to suggest that it was OK to bend the rules once in a while. That she could leave them alone. That she could let them in.

Caitlin stared at her, wondering if it was working. The woman continued to stare angrily back. It didn't seem to be working.

"Thank you for informing us," Caitlin said to her sweetly. "It was so nice meeting you. We are so grateful that you are going to bend the rules for us, just this once, and let us tour the house ourselves."

The woman stared back.

"I didn't say that!" she snapped.

But Caitlin breathed deeply, and closed her eyes, focusing.

She opened them, and stared right at her.

After two full seconds, the woman's eyes began to glaze over. Finally, she said, "You know what…I guess there's no harm in bending the rules once in a while. You two have fun."

The woman turned and walked away, and was soon out of sight.

Caitlin turned to Caleb, elated. She was shocked at her own powers, and so proud of herself. Caleb smiled.

"Only use it when you have to," he cautioned, "and only in a way that will never harm others. This is what separates the benevolent vampire race from the evil."

Caitlin extracted the small, silver key, excited to try it. She tried the lock on the front door, but it didn't work.

"It doesn't fit," she said.

Caleb took it and tried it himself.

He finally furrowed his brow in frustration. "You're right." He looked around. "Maybe there's another entrance."

They walked around to the back of the house, and found another door. Caleb tried the key. It didn't fit there, either.

"Maybe it's not to a door," Caitlin said. "Maybe it's a key to something else. Something *inside* the house."

"Well, I guess we have no choice," he said, then, after looking furtively around, reached up and broke the handle. So much for preservation.

They quickly entered the house and shut the door behind them.

The house was dim, lit only by the exterior light filtering through the small windows. The ceilings were low, and Caleb had to nearly crouch as he walked. It was all wood: wood ceilings, wooden posts, wooden beams, and wide plank, wooded floors. The center of the room was made up of a huge, brick fireplace.

The house was perfectly preserved, and it was like walking into 1672.

They walked around, the floorboards creaking, examining every nook and crevice. They also pored over all the furniture. But Caitlin couldn't find anything in which the key could fit. In fact, she couldn't find any hiding places at all.

They each circled the house, and met in the middle.

"Anything?" Caleb asked.

She shook her head. "You?"

He shook his, too.

Suddenly there was a noise, and they both spun around.

The front door to the house opened, and a large, black man, 50s, stood in the doorway. He took several steps in.

He stopped before Caleb and stared.

Caleb stared back.

"Caleb?" the man finally asked.

Caleb's expression softened.

"Roger?" Caleb asked.

The man broke into a smile, as did Caleb, and they both embraced in a huge hug. They held it for several seconds.

Who is this? Caitlin thought.

Roger began to laugh—a deep, warm, generous laugh. He held Caleb by the shoulders and looked at him. Caleb was a big man, but even so, Roger towered over him.

"Son of a bitch," Roger said. "I haven't seen you in what…a hundred and fifty years?"

"More like 200," Caleb said.

They both stared at each other, surprised. Whoever he was, this had clearly been an important man in Caleb's life.

Caleb turned, and held his hand out to Caitlin. "Excuse my manners," he said. "Roger, may I introduce Caitlin Paine."

Roger did a half bow. "A pleasure to meet you, Caitlin."

Caitlin smiled back. "A pleasure to meet you, too. How do you guys know each other?"

"Oh," Roger said, smiling, "let's just say we go way back."

"Roger is one of my oldest friends," Caleb said. "He's saved my life once or twice."

"More times than that," Rogers said, laughing.

Rose peeked her head out of Caitlin's jacket, and Roger's eyes lit up. "Well, hello little fella," he said, coming over and petting her.

Rose licked his huge palm.

"How did you know we were here?" Caleb asked.

"Caleb, please," Roger said, as if the answer were obvious. "This is an island. Your scent has nowhere to go. It's visible from miles away."

"So you knew the second I got off the boat," Caleb said, smiling. "And you waited to see where I'd go."

"Of course," Roger said. "Wouldn't you? But I would have guessed it would be here." Caleb looked carefully over the room. "Why?"

"There's only one reason one of us comes to the Vincent House. The sword, right? Isn't that what you're after?"

Caitlin and Caleb looked at each other.

"We might be," Caleb said warily.

Roger smiled.

"You know, the thing about that sword," he said, "is that only the person *meant* to find it will. As in, The *One*. I know you're not The One. And as for your friend, with all due respect...well, I don't mean to make any assumptions, but unless she—"

Caitlin reached into her pocket and held out the small, silver key.

Roger stared at if for several second, speechless.

His jaw dropped.

"My god," he said, in a whisper.

He looked at Caleb, as if for confirmation, and Caleb nodded back.

He exhaled.

"Well," he said, humbled, in an entirely different tone, "this does change everything."

He looked Caitlin over. He shook his head.

"I never would have guessed," he said.

"So then...you know where it is?" Caleb asked.

Roger nodded. "Not here," he said.

Caitlin and Caleb exchanged a glance.

"That key," he said, "was accurate at one time. But not anymore. It's a decoy. The Vincent House is no longer the place you'll find it in. Now it's just the place you need to go."

Caitlin was thoroughly confused.

"But—" she began.

"The Vincent House was moved," Roger clarified. "Don't you know its history?"

Caitlin shook her head.

"Caleb. I'm disappointed in you you're slipping," Roger chided. "It used to be in a different location. But 200 years ago, we moved it, to where it is now. The Council got worried about safekeeping. So they moved the object out of the house, and put it in a safer, more stable place. And they assigned someone to guard it. As in, me."

Caleb studied his friend.

"I've been waiting for someone to arrive with that key for almost 200 years," he said. He shook his head again. "I never dreamt it would be you."

"Will you show us?" Caleb asked.

The man looked long and hard at Caleb, then at Caitlin.

He finally held out his huge palm, towards Caitlin.

"May I see that?" he asked.

Caitlin look to Caleb. He nodded.

She reached out and placed the small, silver key into his huge palm.

Roger stared at it. He held it up to the light. He turned it over read the inscription on the back. He finally shook his head.

"God damn," he said. "I was sure it would be bigger."

NINETEEN

Samantha, in the passenger seat, looked over and was impressed by how Sam handled the car. Not bad for someone his age. She was surprised by how well he handled the stick, and she forgave him his initial grinding of gears. He was actually pretty good once he got past third. She liked his aggression, especially when the speedometer hit 120. He had spirit, she had to give him that.

She leaned back, relaxing and enjoying the ride. It was a lot slower than flying, but not bad for human travel. She thought of the man who'd owned this car, that real estate broker—her morning meal—and smiled. His blood still ran through her veins, and it felt good. She was sated.

She didn't need to let the kid drive, but she figured his days were numbered anyway, so why not let him enjoy them, go out with a bang? It would only be a matter of hours now until she'd meet his father, and find out where that sword was. After that, she could dispose of them both.

But something gnawed at her. She was actually starting to like this kid. And that bothered her more than anything else. She couldn't remember liking a human in hundreds of years. Much less a stupid teenager. But, she had to admit, there was something about him. Some kind of kindred spirit, something she recognized. Even at his young age, she could tell he had been kicked around. He had a quality of recklessness, of not caring about the world, of knowing his days were numbered, of being ready to go out in style. And she liked that. It reminded her of an affair she'd had once with a young prince in Bulgaria, in the 1300s...

Maybe she didn't need to kill him right away. Maybe she could keep him alive a bit longer. Take him along for the ride. Maybe, even, keep him alive after she found the sword. She could enslave him. He could be a plaything, to do with as she wished. Maybe even...

She stopped her line of thought, mad at herself. Was she getting soft?

She had to focus on the task ahead. His father. They would be there shortly, within the hour. If he was one of hers, was of the vampire race, she might be in for a fight, as he would sense her presence immediately. She had to be on guard as they pulled up.

She would do whatever it took, fight to the death if need be. This vampire was the key to the sword, the key to her coven's victory. She would go to heaven or hell to make sure they got it.

*

As Sam drove, getting closer, letting the car's navigation system direct him to his Dad's address, he was confused. He had pictured his father living in a upscale town, off of a cool road, on a huge property in an awesome house.

But as the GPS announced that they were close, within a mile or so, Sam felt like something must be wrong. They were driving through a dump of a town—not even a town, really, but just a stretch of dumpy country road, with small, ranch trailers spread out here and there.

When the GPS announced that this was their last turn, Sam couldn't believe his eyes. They drove under a huge sign that read: "Homestead Trailer Park."

This was where his dad lived. In a trailer park.

As he slowly drove down the dirt road, past the spread out trailers, each one looking worse than the next, Sam began to feel a pit in his stomach, the familiar feeling of his dreams about to get crushed. He had been so stupid to get his hopes up. What an idiot he'd been.

The further he got, the more spread out the trailers were, and as he reached the end of a dead end, he saw the number on a light-blue, vinyl trailer, and realized he'd found it. The tiny mobile home was dilapidated. The screen door was crooked on its hinges, the small stairs were cracked, and the lawn was overgrown with knee-high weeds. The home was set back, and hidden from the others by a large clump of bushes. It was private. But not the kind of privacy Sam had imagined.

Sam felt embarrassed. He was so embarrassed to have brought Samantha to this place, and to be introducing her to his Dad. He wished he could just take off, or just curl up and die.

He parked, and killed the engine, and they both sat there. They kind of looked at each other. Sam checked the navigation system for the tenth time to make sure it was the right address. It was.

"Are we getting out?" Samantha finally asked.

Sam didn't really know what to do. What kind of man could live in such a place? What kind of Dad did he come from?

He wanted to just turn the engine, step on the gas, and keep going. But he couldn't.

Sam swallowed hard, opened the door and got out, and Samantha followed.

The two of them approached the house. They took two steps up, the rotted wood stairs sinking, and he pulled back the creaking screen door.

Sam took a deep breath, reached up, and knocked.

There came a bang, and then a rustling inside. Seconds later, the door opened.

And there, across from him, stood his father.

TWENTY

Roger led them back onto the brick walkway, through the manicured grounds, and past the Daniel Fisher House. They exited back on the street, made a quick turn, and then, before they knew it, he was leading them up the front steps and into the huge, historic whaling church.

Caleb and Caitlin looked at each other in wonder. They had just walked by it.

The door was locked, but Roger had the key. He unlocked it, and held it open for them.

"We didn't move it far," he said, with a smile and a wink.

They entered, and he closed and locked the door behind them.

Caitlin was taken aback as they entered the church. It was breathtaking. So light and airy, so beautiful in its simplicity, it was unlike any church she had ever been in. There were no crosses, no religious figures, no ornamentation, not even any columns or beams—it was just a huge open room, lined in every direction with old windows. There were rows and rows of simple, wooden pews, enough to hold hundreds of people. It was a very peaceful place.

"This is the largest open-ceilinged room in America," Rogers said. "No columns, no beams. Master shipbuilders built this place. And it still stands as well today as it did back then."

"So is this how you spend your days now, Roger?" Caleb asked, smiling. "Looking after an old church?"

Roger smiled. "It beats getting you out of trouble," he said. Then he sighed, a long, tired sigh. "I'm tired, Caleb. I've been around a lot longer than you are, and I've just about had enough. I like this place. It's quiet. I don't bother anyone, and no one bothers me. I'm tired of all these god damn wars all the time. Covens, politics....I like being on my own. I like this place.

"And more importantly, I get to look after it. Honestly, after all these years, I didn't think anyone would come along. I was starting to believe that there was no such thing as The One. But I guess I was wrong." Roger looked at Caitlin. "And now you've put me out of a job."

Roger turned to Caleb. "Before I bring you, there's one thing I want to ask of you," he said, looking at Caleb.

Caitlin wonder what it could be, what the price would be for admission to such a valuable object, something that this man had guarded his entire life.

Caleb looked back. "Anything, old friend," he said.

"It's been so long since I've heard you play," Roger said.

He turned and gestured towards an old, grand piano sitting in the corner of the room.

"The Pathétique. Second movement. Just like in Vienna."

Caleb surveyed the piano. He hesitated.

"It's been a long time, Roger."

Roger smiled wide. "I'm sure you still got it."

Caitlin suddenly realized that there was so much about Caleb she didn't know—so much she would probably never know. She felt so young in comparison. She realized that Caleb and Roger had experienced more over the centuries than she and Caleb probably ever would. It saddened her. She so badly wanted to be immortal—a full, true vampire, just like him, by his side forever.

She watched as Caleb walked slowly across the empty church, the floorboards creaking beneath his black leather boots. He took three steps up onto the wooden platform and walked across it, all the way to the corner. He pulled the cover off the Steinway piano, and sat.

He lifted the lid, and stared.

He closed his eyes, and sat there. Caitlin wondered what he was thinking, what sort of memories it was evoking for him. And then, after several moments of silence, she wondered if he'd change his mind, if he wouldn't play after all.

He finally reached up with his hands, and began to play.

And it was beautiful.

The notes echoed throughout the huge, empty church, reverberating off the walls, filling the empty space. It seemed to bounce off of everything.

Caitlin had never heard music like this. Nothing even remotely like this. It made her want to capture the moment. And it made her want to cry.

At that moment, she felt profoundly sad, as it struck her, again, that there was so much about Caleb that she would probably never know. She would just have to accept that she knew as much as she did, and learn to be happy to be with him for the short time that she was.

It also saddened her, as it made her think of Jonah. She hadn't thought of him in so long. When she was with Caleb, she felt no need to think of him. But he was still there, somewhere deep in her consciousness, even from just the short time they'd spent together, and a part of her still felt badly for ending it so abruptly. Whatever they'd had together, it felt unresolved.

A part of her felt that someday they would see each other again. She didn't know how, but she just knew that they would.

Not that she even wanted to. Especially at this moment. She felt wholeheartedly devoted to Caleb, and she hoped that would never change.

The music filled her soul as she stood there for what felt like forever, listening. Neither she nor Roger moved. They both stood there, frozen in silence, as Caleb played perfectly.

Finally, it was over. The final note hung in the air for several seconds, and Caitlin looked over and saw Roger slowly open his eyes.

Caleb got up slowly, walked across the stage, down the steps, and back towards them. He stopped a few feet in front of Roger, and looked at him.

Roger took a deep breath, reached up, and wiped a tear from his eye.

"Exactly as I remembered," Roger said.

He took a deep breath, turned his back, and walked quickly down the hall.

"Follow me," he said

*

They followed Roger across the creaking wood floors and up an old, winding wood staircase. They reached the mezzanine level, and Caitlin look down, and was taken aback by the beauty of the church from this perspective.

They followed Roger down a hall, through a hidden door, and up yet another circular wooden staircase. They continued to follow as they winded higher and higher. Caitlin had the feeling that no one had been up this high in years.

The staircase ended in a small cupola, all the way at the very top of the church, barely big enough to hold the three of them.

Roger reached over to a part of the wall, and gently pulled at a hidden latch. A secret compartment opened, and he extracted a small, jeweled chest.

He held it gingerly in his hands, looking at it sentimentally.

"I never opened it myself," he said. "I've never even seen it open. And I never thought I would. Until I saw your key."

He looked directly at Caitlin. It was hot and airless in the small room, and she was beginning to feel claustrophobic. Dizzy. Everything felt so surreal. And it never seemed to end.

"I knew your father well," he said.

Caitlin's jaw dropped. She was practically speechless. There were so many questions she wanted to ask, she barely knew where to begin.

"What was he like?" was all she could think of.

"Fine man. A great man. I loved him. He was bigger than all of us, bigger than the race. He'd be proud of you for getting this far," he said, as he held out the chest with both hands.

Caitlin reached out and inserted the silver key, heart pounding, praying it would fit. It did.

It slid in with a precious click. She turned it gently to the right, and the lid opened.

All three of them leaned over, anxious to see what was inside.

They were shocked by what they found.

TWENTY ONE

"Hey buddy, move out!" came the gruff voice.

Kyle felt himself being kicked, then nudged with a baton.

He opened his eyes.

He was lying on a cold, hard surface, but had no idea where. Sunlight was creeping over the horizon, and it burned his eyes and skin.

"Hey buddy, did you hear me? I said move it!" the cop yelled.

Kyle opened his eyes fully now, and realized he'd been lying on marble. On the cold, marble steps of City Hall. He was outside, at daybreak, lying sprawled out, like a bum. He looked up and saw two uniformed policeman standing over him, poking and prodding him with their batons, smiling at each other.

Kyle tried to remember what happened, how he'd got here. He remembered reporting to Rexius. Then being grabbed, being tied down. Then, the acid. He reached up and felt one side of his face, and it felt normal. Then he reached up and felt the other—and the pain came flooding back. He could feel the contours, the horrible scars, the disfiguration. They had branded him with Ioric acid. A punishment reserved for traitors. He, Kyle, the man who had been loyal to his coven for thousands of years. For one small mistake. It was unthinkable.

Kyle felt the pain welling up on the side of his face, and rage began to well within him.

"Want to bring him in?" one cop asked the other.

"Nah. Too much paperwork. Let's spare ourselves the aggravation and take care of it ourselves."

One of the cops raised his baton, preparing to bring it down hard.

"Hold him up," he said to the other.

One cop roughly grabbed Kyle by the arm and yanked him to his feet. As he did, the other side of Kyle's face was revealed, and the cops could see the horrible scarring and disfiguration. They both recoiled at the site.

"Holy shit," one cop said. "What the hell is that?"

Rage flooded Kyle, and before the cops could react, he snapped to it, grabbing each, with a single hand, by the chest, and raising each high above his head. They were big men, but Kyle was bigger—much bigger—and much, much stronger. He raised each higher and higher, and before they could react, he pulled them back and then brought them together, smashing into each other.

They both collapsed to the steps, and Kyle stepped up and stomped on their heads, killing each of them.

Kyle's rage continued to well. His own people. They had cast him out like a nobody, like a nothing. After all he had done for them. After he had unleashed the war. All for a small mistake. For that stupid girl. Caitlin. He would make her pay.

But first, he would make his own people pay. No one treated him like that. No one. They might have exiled him, but he didn't have to accept it. After all, there were still vampires loyal to him. He could be the leader of the coven himself.

As he stood there, quaking with rage, it struck him. A plan. A way to get his revenge. A way to take back control. A way to become supreme leader himself.

He thought of the sword. If he had it, if he could find it before they did, he would have the power. Not them. Then he could come back and destroy them. At least those who had betrayed him. Those who'd been loyal, he'd take in as soldiers.

Yes, there would be bloodshed unlike any they had ever seen. And when he finished taking back control, he'd turn to the humans and finish the war himself. The plague would have done its damage by then, and he, Kyle would be in charge. With that sword, he could rule New York. Then all the councils, and all the covens across the world, would have to answer to him.

Yes, he liked the plan. But if he wanted that sword, he'd have to find that girl. Caitlin. And to find her, he would need help. That Russian boy. The singer. The one she turned. The one who still had her scent in his veins.

Yes. A plan was coming to him.

Kyle turned and ran up the steps of City Hall, tearing off the iron locks with one hand as he kicked in the door. The early morning lobby was empty, and he sprinted across the corridor. He reached the far end, pulled back a hidden latch, and a wall opened up. He hurried down the stone staircase, and into the blackness.

Kyle ran full speed, knowing that he could find himself up against an army, but also knowing that they would never expect him to attack by himself. He also knew that they were preoccupied with the war, and that if he hurried, he might be able to get in just long enough to get what he needed. Especially at daybreak, when many of them were settling in for sleep.

Kyle reached the lower levels and ran with all his speed down the hall, until he found the huge door he was looking for. There was only one guard standing outside it, as he suspected— a young and weaker vampire, only hundreds of years old. Before he could react, Kyle had already struck him cleanly across the jaw, knocking him out cold.

Kyle put his shoulder to the door and knocked it in. He crossed the room, and there he was. That Russian boy. Chained to the wall, hands outstretched, mouth gagged, eyes open wide with fear and terror. They'd had him in there for days, and by now, this boy had been utterly broken. Kyle ran across the room, not wasting time, and tore off his hand and foot chains. The boy reached up and pulled off the duct tape from his mouth and began shouting.

"Who are you? Why am I here? Where are you taking me? Why did—"

Kyle reached up and backhanded him with enough strength to knock him out. Then he slung him over his shoulder and carried him out the room, chains dragging.

He sprinted with him through the empty corridor and up the staircase, and before he knew it, he was out the door, through City Hall, and into the daylight. He ran for all he was worth, and was pleased to realize that no one was following him.

He relaxed a bit, as he ran. He had what he needed. This boy, with Caitlin's blood still in his veins, could lead him right to her. And where she was, the sword would follow.

He smiled. It was only a matter of time. Soon he would have the sword.

TWENTY TWO

Caitlin and Caleb flew over miles of dark woods as they crossed Martha's Vineyard, heading into the late afternoon sun. She marveled at how big the island was. She had imagined it to be a small place, but as she looked down, she realized that it was massive. The Aquinnah cliffs, where they were heading, were on the far corner of the island, all the way on the other side. Even flying at Caleb's speed, it would take a while.

Caleb didn't like to fly if other people were around, as he never wanted to draw undue attention to him or to the race. But the island was so deserted this time of year, that he had no qualms about flying them from one side to the other, especially over a patch of woods.

Caitlin's mind spun as she thought of the whaling church, and of the latest clue they'd found. It was not at all what she'd expected. She had guessed it might be another key. Instead, they'd found a scroll—a brittle, yellowing parchment, and torn in half, right down the middle. It had been obvious, from first glance, that the other half of it was missing, and that without it, the first half would be useless. Half of a riddle. Given its condition, it was amazing it had survived, and she was sure it would not be preserved if it hadn't been stored inside a narrow, metal, airproof container—one which she now felt bulging snugly in her pocket.

The three of them had scrutinized the cryptic message on the half of the scroll, knowing even as they did that it would be useless. There were words and phrases which were torn down the middle. Fragments. Pieces of a riddle. It read:

The Four Horsemen...
They leave...
Enter a ring...
Meet at...
And find the...
Beside the fourth...

They had guessed again and again, trying to complete the sentences. But try as they did, they could not decipher it without the other half.

They had all felt deflated, and Roger had seemed apologetic. There were no hints, no leads whatsoever as to where the other half of the scroll might be.

So Caitlin and Caleb had decided to go to the only other lead they had: the Aquinnah Cliffs. Her dream.

Caitlin struggled to remember the dream, and it already felt distant, hazy, as if she'd dreamt it months ago. She started to worry if she'd even dreamt it at all. She didn't want to let Caleb down, or lead him any deeper on this wild goose chase.

As they turned the bend, the woods below them opened up, and the landscape changed to beautiful, tall grass, swaying in the wind. It was lit up by the late afternoon sun, and glowed a soft red. It was beautiful. Below, she saw a farm, random sheep and cows spread out on the primitive landscape.

Soon Caitlin could smell the salt air, and as they rounded another bend, the landscape shifted to dune grass, then to sand.

Then, the cliffs came into view.

They were breathtaking. Hundreds of feet high, their sand glowed with a mystical red color. Especially in the late afternoon sun, it looked as if these huge cliffs were alive, on fire.

At their base was a soft, sandy ocean beach, littered with rocks of all shapes and sizes. Amidst these were occasional boulders, sitting haphazardly on the sand and out into the crashing waves. They look prehistoric. The entire place like magical, like a beach set on Mars. She couldn't even fathom that such a place existed.

Rose must have sensed it, too, because she, still tucked into Caitlin's jacket, peeked out her head and looked, sniffing the salt air.

As they circled the cliffs, slowing, coming in for a landing, something about them struck Caitlin as familiar. She definitely felt as if she had been here before. Yes. This was the place she. More importantly, she seemed to remember being here with her Dad at some point.

She didn't know if they would find anything, but she felt as if they were exactly where they were meant to be.

The beach was empty, entirely theirs. They set down softly, Caleb gently landing on the sand, and Caitlin let Rose down. Rose ran in the sand, jumped into the water, then ran back to the shore as the water crashed on her.

Caitlin and Caleb smiled.

They walked slowly down the beach, taking it all in. They walked in silence, as Caleb reached out and took her hand.

The beach was dominated by the sound of the crashing waves, and smell of the ocean air. Caitlin closed her eyes and breathed deeply. It felt so refreshing.

Caleb scanned the cliffs, the beach, the rocks. So did she.

"This is definitely the place," Caitlin said. "I feel like I was here with him."

Caleb nodded. "It would make sense. This is a very powerful place for our race."

Caleb looked at him in surprise. "Have you been here before?" she asked.

"Many times," he answered. "The Aquinnah Cliffs are one of our sacred places, one of the oldest energy fields on earth. The red clay and sand store and discharge ancient energy, which restores us.

"Humans, of course, don't realize. They have never understood the exact meaning of this place. But we have known for thousands of years. It is a place of power. A mystical place. One created by the ancients.

"It would make sense for your father to bring you here. It is a rite of passage for all vampires. A place where we bring our young, or those who have been turned. Primarily, though, it is a place of love."

Caitlin looked at him. "Love?" she asked.

"Vampire weddings are very rare," he continued, "because we cannot procreate, and because committing for eternity is not something we choose lightly. But when two vampires marry, the ceremonies are very elaborate and sacred. They can go one for days. And nearly always, this is the place they happen."

Caitlin looked around, in awe.

"If we were to come here at night, especially on a full moon," he said, "you would likely find a vampire wedding ceremony. It is a place of matrimony, as these rocks symbolize eternity.

They are among the oldest elements on this planet. It is believed that their energy charges the union with a bond that can never be broken."

Caitlin felt her heart swell with his words. Although they'd been together a short time, she already felt like she knew him forever. As he spoke of the ceremony, of marriage, she realized that there was nothing she'd like more than to be assured that she could spend the rest of her life with him. It depressed her that her life would end before his, that they were of two different races, that their love was forbidden. That she would be just another memory for him.

She wanted to tell him all this, but she didn't know what to say, exactly, or how to express herself. And she didn't know if he felt the same way about her. So she just kept walking, silently.

Everything felt so perfect, just the way it was right now. Why couldn't things stay this way? She loved this island, this beach. She could see herself staying here, settling here with Caleb. She could see them building a life together, safe from the rest of the world, at peace. Maybe they'd build a small house, high up on the cliffs, overlooking the ocean. They could leave their pasts behind, start over. Was that even possible?

Over the last weeks, Caitlin had felt so out of control of her life. She had felt events happening all around her, felt herself being swept up in everything. But now that things had quieted a bit, now that their trail had seemingly come to a dead end, she wondered if they could stop searching. She wondered if things could actually return to some semblance of normal.

A part of her, deep down, knew that it was impossible. She knew that, no matter what they did, they were both rushing headlong into destiny. Into their fate. And that, very soon, things between them would change forever. It depressed her.

She found herself thinking of Caleb's piano playing, of how beautiful the music had been. It's notes rang in her ears.

"I didn't know you could play the piano," she said softly.

He sighed. "It's been many years. I'm afraid I didn't do the piece justice. You should've heard Ludwig play it."

She looked at him, shocked. "Do you mean Ludwig…as in Beethoven?" she asked, dumbfounded.

He nodded.

"You heard Beethoven play that? Personally?"

"Yes," he said. "Towards the end of his life."

She was flabbergasted. It shocked her to consider what he must have seen.

"So, then…you met him?" she asked

198

"Yes," Caleb said. "He was a close friend. He was one of us."

"A *vampire?*" Caitlin asked, shocked.

Caleb simply nodded.

Caitlin wanted to know more—she wanted to know everything—but she could see that Caleb didn't want to talk about it. Whatever had happened, it held deep feelings for him.

"It must be so incredible to have met people like that. To remember things like that," she said.

"Sometimes," he said. "More often, it's a burden."

"Why?"

"After time, memories begin to weigh you down. You get so lost in past events, it becomes hard to live in the present. It's like a house filled with old things. After a certain point, there's no room to bring in anything new."

They walked in silence for several minutes. The sun was beginning to set, and it cast a soft light over everything. The waves crashed, Rose yelped as she ran by their feet, and some passing seagulls screech overhead.

Caitlin looked around, wondering if there was any clue, any trace of her father, anything that she remembered. But she couldn't find a thing.

She heard a loud noise, and felt a breeze, and suddenly, two white horses raced past them. She turned to look, to see where they had come from, but there was nothing anywhere in sight. Wild horses. They galloped right past them, down the beach, running in the shallow water.

Caleb and Caitlin turned and looked at each other at the same time. It was amazing. Unlike anything she had ever seen.

"Wild horses," he said. "And white. An excellent sign. Let's catch them!" he said, and took off at a sprint.

Caitlin at first thought he was crazy: how could they possibly catch up with a horse? But then she remembered her newfound speed, and she ran.

Caitlin felt her legs running for her. Before she knew it, she was racing faster than she had ever thought possible. She caught up to Caleb, and the two of them sped up, and within seconds, they were running alongside the horses. Rose ran right behind them.

Caleb smiled wide. "Let's ride!" he screamed.

He jumped onto the back of one of them, and Caitlin followed suit, running as fast as she could, and leaping in the air onto the back of the other.

She couldn't believe it, but she was now riding on the back of this horse, beside Caleb. He was laughing, his hair blowing wildly in the wind. The two of them raced down the beach, side-by-side, racing further and further into the sunset. She couldn't believe that she was able to do this, to hang on. It all felt too surreal.

The horses took them down the beach, for miles. As they went, they got a bird's-eye view of the cliffs, the rocks, the sand. Caitlin was surprised to see just how huge this beach was. It seemed to stretch forever.

And then suddenly, without warning, the horses came to an abrupt stop.

No matter how much prodding Caleb and Caitlin did, they refused to move.

Caitlin and Caleb exchanged glances, puzzled.

"I guess they want to let us off here!" Caleb yelled, laughing.

Caitlin looked down and saw that the horses were standing in the ocean, in knee-high water.

Caleb smiled wide. "Guess we'll have to get a little wet!"

He jumped down, landing in the knee-high water.

Caitlin took off her shoes, holding them in one hand, and followed.

The water was freezing on her bare feet, but it only came up to her shins as the wave receded. And it actually felt refreshing on her bare feet, as did the soft sand.

She looked up and saw the horses galloping away, down the empty beach, towards the sun.

Rose ran along the sand, testing the waves, then running back to the sand again, yelping.

Caleb came over, grabbed Caitlin, and playfully picked her up as a wave came in, keeping her dry. He was so strong, the wave crashed into his legs, and it didn't even budge him. He was like a rock. He held her close, hugging her, keeping her dry, laughing and smiling, as he whirled her around.

She felt her heart swell.

As he gently lowered her, holding her tight, she looked into his eyes, and he looked into hers. Their eyes locked. Slowly, his smile faded. His expression turned more serious. Turned to something else.

She saw his eyes change color, from brown to a sea-green. He stared down at her, right back into her eyes, and they both felt the same thing at the same moment.

Her heart pounded, as he leaned in and kissed her.

*

It was a kiss of one thousand suns. Her body filled with a warmth and tingling unlike anything she had ever experienced. She kissed him back, more forcefully, and soon he was holding her, picking her up out of the water, and walking her towards the shore.

He brought her to the dry sand, and they lay down together, on the empty beach, with seemingly the entire world to themselves. Their kisses became more passionate, and she reached up and ran her hand through his hair.

She had been imagining this moment from the first time she met him.

She had never loved anyone as much as this.

TWENTY THREE

As Sam stood there, facing his father, his heart sank. He couldn't believe it. While he'd been disappointed by the trailer park, by the mobile home, by the unkempt surroundings, nothing had prepared him for his disappointment upon seeing his Dad. All of his dreams came crashing down at once.

His dad was a short, thin, frail man, maybe in his 50s, balding badly, with long stringy hair that draped down over one side of his head. He hadn't shaved in days, and it looked like he'd slept in his clothes. His skin was covered in warts, and scarred by bad acne. He had small, beady black eyes, which darted about in his head. He stared back at Sam, looking not unlike a rat. In fact, his entire aura exuded sleaze. And he reeked. He probably hadn't bathed in days.

He looked nothing like Sam. And he looked nothing like the Dad that Sam had imagined he'd come from.

Sam couldn't fathom how he possibly had come from such a human being. He felt worse about himself than he ever had.

Maybe he had the wrong address. He prayed that was the case.

Please, God, let it not be him.

"Sam?" the man suddenly asked.

With that word, that confirmation that he was indeed at the right address, Sam's heart completely sank. It was him.

Sam tried to find his words. "Um, like, are you…"

"Your dad?" he said, trying to smile, revealing rows of small, orange teeth. "That's right."

The man looked from Sam over to Samantha, looking her up and down. He licked his lips.

"I thought you were coming alone?" he asked Sam, looking at Samantha as he said it.

"I…" Sam began, "well, I, um…"

"Who's this?" he asked, still staring at her.

"This is Samantha," Sam said, finally. "She's my…" Sam trailed off, not quite knowing what to call her.

"Girlfriend," Samantha filled in for him, graciously.

Sam was grateful that she had. And he loved the sound of that term, especially coming from her.

"All right, well…" the man said, trailing off. He turned his back and walked inside.

Sam and Samantha looked at each other, both caught off guard by his odd welcome. Neither of them knew what to make of it. Was that an invitation to come inside?

Sam stepped tentatively inside, Samantha close behind.

Before she closed the door, she looked both ways carefully, and then closed the door firmly and locked it.

*

Samantha surveyed the small, darkened mobile home. The blinds were all drawn, and the room was lit only by a small lamp in the corner. It was a nice sunny day, but you'd never know it in here. It was a gloomy home, and packed with clutter.

The instant she'd met this man, Samantha had sensed that he was not one of them, not a vampire. She would have known. This told her that Sam's father was not the vampire—that his *mother* was. That they had been searching for the wrong line of his lineage. They were wasting their time with this man—unless he could lead them to Sam's real mom.

She could see the obvious disappointment on Sam's face, and she actually felt sorry for him. She couldn't remember how long it had been since she'd actually felt sorry for a human, and she chided herself. This kid was really throwing her off guard.

"So, well…" the man began, obviously socially awkward. He paced around his place, barely looking at them. "What are you drinking?" he finally asked. "Want a beer?"

Sam paused. "Um, like…whatever is fine," he said.

The man went to his tiny kitchen, and returned shortly with two tall cans of warm Schlitz. He set them down on the coffee table. Neither Sam nor Samantha touched them.

She could see Sam standing there, fidgeting, and that he didn't know what to say. And that his Dad didn't, either.

An awkward silence fell over the room. Something was very odd. His dad didn't seem that happy to see them. Either that, or he was just very socially awkward.

Samantha looked around, surveying what she could see of the place. There was clutter everywhere, and it was completely unkempt. Empty soda cans littered the floor, alongside stacks of newspapers and magazines. There was a small desk in the far corner, and she could see his laptop was open.

Samantha sensed something, and she used her vampire vision to zoom in, across the room, onto the details of the screen. She could see that he was logged on to Facebook. And under a different account name.

"So, like, did you tell anyone you were coming to visit?" his Dad finally asked.

Sam stared back at him, puzzled. "Uh, like—"

"Like did you tell your mom you're coming to see me?"

"No," Sam answered. "I haven't talked to her in a while. This was all, like, spur of the moment. I just thought, like, it would be cool to meet."

The man nodded. He seemed to relax a bit.

"Well good, yeah," the man said. He reached into his pocket and took a crumpled packet of cigarettes and lit one. He dragged on it, filling the small room with smoke. "So, like, what are you guys into?"

Sam and Samantha exchanged a glance, not sure what he meant.

"Um, like…what do you mean?" Sam asked.

Samantha turned back to the laptop, and zoomed in again on the Facebook page. Something about it was bothering her. She looked closely, at the entire screen, and could see that there were several tabs open up at once. All on Facebook. And all under different user names.

His Dad must have seen her looking, because at that moment, he suddenly walked over and shut his laptop. He turned back to them.

"I mean," he said, "you guys, like...are you having sex with each other?" he asked.

Samantha saw him suddenly reach over and grab something off the table.

She looked over and saw the confusion on Sam's face, and then saw the anger starting to cloud over it.

At that moment, she realized. This was not his Dad at all. It was an imposter. An internet predator. A pedophile. Luring people in on Facebook. Fishing for different kids. Waiting for someone to come along like Sam, someone desperate, just eager enough to be willing to believe this might be his Dad.

The man was quick. Before Samantha could react, he had grabbed a large kitchen knife, darted across the room, and grabbed Sam in a chokehold from behind. He held the huge knife tightly against Sam's throat, pushing into it hard enough to almost draw blood.

Sam's eyes watered over in shock and pain.

"Make a move, and he's dead," the man said to Samantha, in a fierce voice.

This was an interesting situation for Samantha. Given that this man was not Sam's father, she had no more business here, and was just wasting her time. She could just walk out and let Sam die. It wouldn't make a difference. This was the only lead he'd had, and now Sam was useless to her.

But there was something that made her hesitate. A spark of something she was starting to feel for the kid. She couldn't believe it, but a part of her was actually starting to care about him. And if there was anything she hated more than humans, it was human creeps like this guy. No, she couldn't just walk out.

"Get down on your knees and take off your shirt," the man ordered Samantha in a dark, steely voice, as he held the knife to Sam's throat.

Sam tried to squirm, but the man held even more tightly, starting to draw a bit of blood.

Samantha could kill the man at any time. But the problem was, he held the knife so tightly, she didn't want to see him kill Sam. She couldn't make any rash moves.

Samantha dropped to her knees, raised her hands, and slowly removed her shirt, revealing her bra.

She looked up and saw the creep's eyes light up, his disgusting grin, ear to ear. He reached out and pointed his knife at her.

"Your bra," he ordered.

Sam must have seen his chance, because at that moment, he moved with admirable speed for a human. He reached up and grabbed the creep's wrist, struggling with all he had.

But the creep was strong. Years of preying on kids had probably built a wiry strength into his frame, had probably prepared him for things like this. As Sam struggled, the creep broke free and sliced Sam's cheek, drawing blood.

Sam screamed out in pain, raising his hands to his cheek. Blood was everywhere.

The creep then pulled the knife back and Samantha could see that he was preparing to plunge it into Sam's chest.

Samantha broke into action. She suddenly leapt across the room, catching the knife in midair and yanking the creep's arm back with enough force to tear it from its socket.

The creep screeched and dropped the knife.

Samantha, not done, reached over, and with her superhuman strength, grabbed his neck and twisted it in one swift motion, breaking it and killing him.

The man slumped, lifeless, to the floor.

Samantha, still coursing with rage, looked over and saw that Sam stood there, eyes wide open, in shock, staring at her. He was so surprised, he looked oblivious to the pain he was in. She was sure he had never witnessed anything like that in his life. And probably never would again.

He had tried, he had really tried, to save her. Even with the knife on his throat. No one had made a gesture for her like that in centuries.

Maybe she would keep him alive, after all.

TWENTY FOUR

When Caitlin and Caleb woke, it was night. They lay on the beach together, on the sand, on the warm night, and under the light of an enormous full moon.

They still had the beach to themselves, and the sound of the crashing waves was all around them. They both lay there, awake, undressed, in each other's arms, using their coats as a makeshift blanket. Rose lay beside them.

They were both changed people.

They stared into each other's eyes. They rolled over and kissed each other again, slowly.

Their relationship had changed forever. She had changed forever. And nothing made her happier.

They were no longer two random people, friends, kept together by the same mission. They were now lovers. A couple. *Together.*

Caitlin only hoped that it would last forever.

There were so many questions she was burning to ask. Like, *what now?* He had crossed a line, forbidden for his race. What if they found him? Would they kill him? Had he risked it all for her? Was she really worth it?

And now that he had, would he leave her? Was there any way for them to stay together, to make it last?

What could their future possibly look like?

She was overcome with emotion, overcome by knowing what he had sacrificed for her.

"I'm afraid," she finally said, softly.

"Of what?" he asked.

"Of us," she said. "Of dying. You will live forever. But I..." She struggled to think how to phrase it. "...I won't," she said. "I want to be with you. I want to be like you. I want to be immortal," she said.

His expression turned somber. He slowly reached over, dressed himself, and stood.

He stared off at the ocean.

She dressed, too, grateful for the warmth of her coat and patting it to make sure her journal and the scroll were still safe inside. She stood beside him.

"I want to be with you, too," he said. "But trust me, you do not want to be immortal. It is a curse. It is much better to die. To start again, clean, fresh, in another lifetime, another place, another time, another body. To not have to remember. To let the life cycle take its course. Our kind...we are unnatural."

He turned and looked at her.

"There is nothing more I would love than to have you by my side. But being with me forever is not worth the pain of immortality."

"*Please*," she said, taking his hand. "It's what I want. Turn me," she said, starting into his eyes. "Turn me so that I can be a true vampire. So that I can be with you forever."

He stared back at her, and his eyes welled up.

"As much as I love you, that I could never do," he said. "You would be stuck in limbo forever. You would never be able to procreate. I could never inflict that on you. Even for selfish reasons. And if I were to turn you without permission, my punishment would be severe."

Her heart fell. Maybe it was not meant to be, after all.

Caleb took her hand silently.

"If we are going to spend the night here, we should find some shelter, build a fire," he said.

He led her as they walked along the cliffs, in silence.

"I thought I saw something earlier, when we were riding," he said. "A cave," he added. "There," he said, pointing.

There was indeed a small cave, set back into the cliff. It was not that deep or wide, but it was enough to provide shelter.

The cave's floor was comprised of the same fine sand as the beach, and it was lit up by the full moon. There was already a large pile of burnt wood sitting in its center. Clearly, others had used this spot before. It was probably a popular spot for bonfires, maybe even for lovers to spend the night.

Caleb reached down and rubbed his hands with lightning speed, as he had done once before, and within seconds, the firewood was lit and burning. Soon, a roaring fire illuminated the cave. Rose came close and lay down beside it.

Caitlin got close, standing beside Caleb and wrapping one arm around his waist, feeling the warmth of the fire.

They both sat down and looked up at the cave, at the ceiling, at the graffiti on its walls. It was shaped in an arch, and the light reflected off it in a million strange ways.

"Where do we go from here?" Caitlin asked.

She was asking about the sword. But she was also asking about *them*.

"I don't know," he said. "We seem to have come to a dead-end."

"I'm sorry," she said. "Maybe my dream…maybe it didn't mean anything. Maybe we followed the trail in the wrong direction. Maybe we need to go back to the Vincent House. Maybe there's something we overlooked, some clue that would point –"

Caleb suddenly put a hand on her arm, stopping her. He was looking up at the walls, scrutinizing them.

She looked up and saw it, too.

He got up, and she followed.

There, in the far corner of the cave, high up, was an indent in the wall, almost in the shape of a cross. It looked surreal, unnatural. They had only seen it because the full moon, and because the fire had burned so strongly. Otherwise, no one could have ever come across this. It was small. And if it hadn't have been for his keen eye, it would have been easily missed.

Caitlin reached up, and scraped away stone and dirt. As she did, the shape became clearer. It was indeed a tiny indent. In the shape of a key.

Caitlin reached into her pocket, and extracted the key the small key to the Vincent house. She held it up and looked at Caleb. He nodded back.

She slipped it inside, and it fit perfectly.

They looked at each other, dumbfounded.

She turned the key, and it clicked. A small compartment open in the wall of the rock.

She reached in and extracted it. It was a scroll. Torn in half.

They both looked at each other, speechless. It was the second half of the scroll.

*

Caitlin reached into her pocket and took out her half of the scroll. She was grateful it was still in its airtight metal container, spared from air and water damage.

They held them both up together and walked closer to the fire, holding them to the light.

As they did, the entire inscription became clear:

The Four Horsemen travel a trail to freedom.
They leave common ground,
Enter a ring of blood,
Meet at the house,
And find the ones they loved
Beside the fourth tip of the cross.

They both looked at each other, in awe that they found it here.

"What does it mean?" she asked.

"I'm…not sure. But these words…a 'trail to freedom,' the 'common'…. I might be mistaken, but I believe it all points to the Freedom Trail. Boston. That would explain the 'trail to freedom.' And the 'common' could be the Boston Common. I don't know where, exactly, it's pointing us, but I would guess it's somewhere on the Freedom Trail. It would make sense Salem, Edgartown, Boston. All three are very strongly connected."

Caitlin struggled to get her mind around this.

"But…how is it possible?" she asked. "It seems so random. Why would we find it here? In this cave? In this place? It doesn't make any sense. What if we had gone somewhere else?"

"But it *does* make sense," he replied. "Think about it. We did not come here by accident. Your father visited you. He led us here. And those horses took us right to this cave and stopped."

She looked at him.

"Horses are a great aid to the vampire race. They are mystical. Messengers. They have been with us from the beginning of time. They came when we needed them. It was no coincidence. They led us here. Sometimes," he continued, "events that seem like a coincidence are the most pre-planned of all."

She stared at the scroll, marveling at the old writing, at the events that brought them here. More than ever, she began to feel that all of this was destined.

And she began to hope that maybe her relationship with Caleb could be destined, too.

"So where now?" she asked. "Boston?"

He nodded. "Looks like we need to get back on that boat."

TWENTY FIVE

Kyle paced the deck of the small yacht, anxious as they sped in the early morning towards Martha's Vineyard. He could not stand still. He hated boats, and he hated water. Worse, he hated crossing water, like most of his kind. Perhaps even more than most.

That Russian boy had insisted that Caitlin was in this direction. So he'd went with him, up the coast, along a highway. But then their search had ended in a harbor. The Russian had pointed out to the ocean. He had insisted that stupid girl, the source of all his trouble, was on the island.

Kyle had gotten into such a rage, he hadn't been able to control himself. Not only had this girl made him chase her up the entire East Coast, not only had she made him miss the war, but now she was forcing him to board a boat, to cross water. He had marched up to the first docked yacht he had seen, leapt on board, and had killed the entire crew on the spot. He'd thrown them all overboard, had hijacked their boat, and he and the Russian had taken off. At least killing them had taken the edge off of his rage.

But now that they were out at sea, surrounded by nothing but blue, his rage flared up again. He had had enough of chasing this girl. He wanted to find her already, kill her, after making her show him exactly where her father was—or where the sword was.

He nearly jumped out of his skin as he paced on deck, wanting the yacht to go faster. He ran up to Sergei, who was steering, and yelled at him again.

"Make it go faster!" he screamed.

"I can't, my master," he pleaded, afraid. "This is as fast as this boat will go."

"You are certain she is on this island?" he asked for the tenth time.

"I am certain that she has crossed water in this direction," he answered. "I feel her scent in my veins."

"That is not what I asked you," Kyle responded, threateningly.

The Russian lifted his head, looking at the air, breathing in. For a moment, he seemed confused. Almost as if he were unsure, or changing his mind. As if he had lost her scent.

If he had, Kyle would kill him.

"I...am sure they came in this direction. I sense their presence strongly. But...that is all I know," he said.

Kyle stormed back to the railing. He face burned red with anger. He was missing it all. After thousands of years of waiting, the war—*his* war—was beginning without him. Right now, back in New York, the plague was beginning to spread. His work, unleashed. And here he was, far away from it all, stuck on a boat with some stupid Russian opera singer. Not able to enjoy it. Not able to watch the pathetic humans screaming, running for their lives. It was the part he had been looking forward to most.

He would really make this girl pay.

Kyle gripped the railing with both of his hands in such a rage that he bent it in half, then tore it completely off the deck.

*

As Caitlin stood on the ferry, holding the railing, the water moving quickly below, Rose tucked into her jacket and Caleb beside her, she looked out at the horizon. She couldn't see land, but she knew it would be coming soon.

A part of her wished she would never see land. As long as they were out at sea, surrounded by blue, things would remain the same. She and Caleb would still be together. But when she spotted the first sign of land, she knew that life would begin, inexorably, to change. Once they reached land, they would be drawn, like a magnet, right into the heart of Boston, onto the Freedom Trail. She just knew that this would be the final stop in their search. She could feel it. And that terrified her.

Apparently Caleb was nervous, too. She looked over and saw him clutching the railing, looking out, and she could see the worry etched in his face. She was beginning to recognize his facial expressions, and she knew that this was not one he wore often. She could see that it was not from his fear of water. It was something else. Was he also afraid of their future? Of what would happen once they found the sword?

They both knew that, once he found it, he couldn't take her with her. He would be on the warpath. Likely, back with his coven, in the midst of a vampire war. She could not see a role for herself in that. And yet she could not see a life without him, either.

Things were different between them now. As he slipped his arm around her waist, and held her close, she realized that she had never felt so close to anyone. It was almost as if they were one mind, looking out of the water. She was a changed woman. And she felt that somehow, even if in a small way, he had been changed by last night, too.

This time, on the ride back, they were both silent. Neither obsessed about the latest clue, neither spent time trying to decipher the riddle, to speculate as to where it might be. They were simply content to stand next to each other, to be with each other. Neither felt the need to talk. It was the calm before the storm, and they both just wanted to enjoy it.

Suddenly, Caleb grimaced. His jaw set hard, the way it sometimes did when he was getting ready to fight.

She looked at him.

"What is it?" she asked.

He stared at the horizon, squinting, clenching his jaw. Several seconds of silence followed.

"I sense something," he said.

She waited for him to add more, but he didn't.

"What?" she asked, finally.

He stared for several more seconds.

"I don't know," he said. "There is a great disturbance. I can feel my people suffering.... I feel...people searching for us. And I feel...we are heading into grave danger."

TWENTY SIX

As their yacht pulled up into the dock in Edgartown, Kyle could wait no longer. He leapt from the deck, flying twenty feet, and landed nimbly on the pier, leaving the Russian to tie up the boat.

On dry land, he felt better already.

The Russian was quick to follow, killing the engine, anchoring the yacht, and hurrying to catch up.

"Hey, you can't dock your boat there!" yelled a middle-aged, potbellied man with bright red cheeks, storming up to them. "That dock is private! It's reserved for—"

Before the man could finish, Kyle grabbed him with one hand by the throat, and squeezed with such force, that he lifted the heavy man off the ground by several feet, dangling him in the air.

The man's eyes bulged from his head, as his face turned bright red. Kyle grimaced, and then in one motion, threw him off the side of the dock.

The man landed with a splash, far off in the water.

Kyle hope he killed him. He should have squeezed longer.

"Where is she?" Kyle demanded through gritted teeth.

The Russian looked nervously about, trying to get his bearings. He raised his nose and checked the air in every direction.

"If you have lost her, I will kill you," Kyle said slowly.

The Russian looked again, and stopped in the direction of Main Street.

"She went this way," he said.

He marched in that direction, Kyle following on his heels.

*

Kyle and Sergei walked up the stairs of the Edgartown whaling church, and without slowing, Kyle kicked in the double doors.

They broke it open with a loud crack, and Kyle marched right through the parlor and into the center of the church, Sergei close behind. They stopped in the middle of the empty room, and looked about.

No one was there.

Kyle reached over and grabbed the Russian by the shoulders.

"I'm tired of this!" he yelled. "WHERE IS SHE!!?"

"Nowhere that you'll ever find," came a cool, collected voice from the back of the church.

Kyle and Sergei both spun around.

There stood Roger, in the entrance, staring back calmly.

Kyle sensed the shift in energy, and knew he was facing one of his own. Finally. No more humans to bother with. They were getting closer.

Kyle walk slowly, Sergei by his side.

"On the contrary," Kyle said, slowly, "you are going to tell me exactly where she is, who she is with, and where she is going," he said, bearing down on Roger.

Roger took a few steps towards them, then suddenly reached back and hoisted something at them.

Kyle saw it coming, but Sergei was not so quick.

Hurling right at them was a long, tapered, vampire spear. Kyle dodged in time, but Sergei did not. The silver-tipped spear grazed his cheek, cutting through skin, tearing open his cheek before continuing on. It was not a direct hit, but enough to draw a lot of blood.

Sergei screamed out in pain, raising his hands to his face, now covered in blood.

Kyle didn't hesitate. He took three steps forward, leapt in the air, and planted a hard kick with both feet right on Roger's chest, sending him flying across the room and crashing into the wall.

Before Roger could get up, Kyle was already on top of him, choking him.

Kyle felt Roger's energy, and he could feel that Roger was one of the old ones. A vampire so old that his strength had greatly diminished. Kyle outmatched him, and knew he could kill him easily. He was going to enjoy torturing him. Slowly.

Kyle saw a sudden movement of Roger's hand, a flash of something yellow, and before he could react, he realized.

Roger had just snuck a suicide pill into his own mouth.

It was too late.

Kyle felt the body go limp in his arms.

In the greatest rage of his life, Kyle threw back his head and screeched, a primal roar that made every windowpane in the church shatter.

TWENTY SEVEN

Sam was still reeling.

That scene inside the mobile home had been so intense, he still couldn't process it. That creep. The knife. The struggle. His cheek. And then Samantha. Killing him like that. It was unbelievable. Who was she?

As he sat in the roadside diner, across from her in a booth, he looked her over. He was more attracted to her than ever—but also wary now. Cautious. She looked totally relaxed, sipping on her vanilla milkshake, and he couldn't understand. Was this the same chick? Here she was, this totally cool and hot, awesome chick, who he loved hanging out with—and yet she had also been that crazy, psycho girl that totally killed that creep without even blinking an eye. Had she really killed him?

It had all gone down so quickly, and the place was so dark, he couldn't even really tell what had happened, exactly. But he remembered the noise, that sickening crack when she twisted his neck. And he remembered seeing the guy hit the ground, totally limp. The dude looked dead to him. But he couldn't say for sure. Maybe she'd just knocked him out. But still. How did she do that? That dude was strong. And he had a knife.

For the millionth time, he hated himself. He had been so stupid. Naïve. How could he have really believed him, have fallen for an internet predator? Was he really such an idiot? What was he thinking? He felt so ashamed. More than anything, he felt more convinced than ever that he'd never find his Dad.

On top of it all, he'd dragged Samantha into it. And worse, he didn't even protect her. She'd had to protect him. How embarrassing. She must think he was a real jerk.

He worried that she'd just take off. He couldn't blame her.

"You OK?" she asked, looking at his cheek.

He remembered, and he reached up, and pulled off the paper towel stuck to his face. He checked it. The bleeding had slowed—but it still hurt like hell.

"Yeah," he said, then looked her over. He noticed she wasn't bruised at all. "So, like, how did you do that back there? I mean, kick that guy's ass?"

She shrugged. "I studied karate most my life. Hope it didn't freak you out. But that guy was dangerous, and I didn't want to take any chances. It was just a really easy move that I did on him. I can teach you."

She had a way of always making him feel better. It was like she knew what he was thinking, and knew how to put him at ease. It was incredible. All of his worries flew out the window.

"I'm really sorry," he said. "I'm such an idiot. I can't believe I took you there."

"Hey," she said, "we wanted to take a drive anyway, right?"

He stared at her, and then they both burst out laughing.

The tension in the air lifted.

Sam reached out, and took a big bite of his untouched burger, and as he did, Samantha suddenly stared at his wrist. She reached up and grabbed it with her icy hands.

Sam lowered the burger in mid-bite, and wondered what she was doing. She pulled his wrist closer to her, and stared at it. His watch. She was staring at his watch.

As she did, her expression changed. She seemed totally serious now. Transfixed.

"What?" he finally asked.

"Where did you get this?" she asked, deadly serious.

He looked at his watch. He had totally forgotten he was even wearing it. He'd always worn it, ever since he was a kid. It was like a part of him, and he didn't even realize when he had it on. It was a weird-looking watch, he had to give her that. But still, he couldn't understand why she was so obsessed with it.

"It was my dad's," he said. "Or at least, I think it was. I was too young to remember. I've always had it."

Sam looked at it himself now, curious. It was encased in some kind of weird metal—he'd always thought it was some kind of platinum—and it had these weird carvings all along the side. It actually looked ancient, and it ticked time in a weird way. It was actually pretty weird that he'd never had to wind it once, or change the battery. It just always ticked, and always told time perfectly.

She ran her fingers along it.

"Here," he said, taking it off. "Go ahead. Check it out. Try it on, if you want. There's this really cool stuff on the back. I was never able to figure out what it meant," he said, handing it to her.

She look like a kid in a candy store as he placed it on her palm. She turned it over, and looked at it carefully, and her eyes opened wide. She seemed genuinely surprised.

"What is it? Can you read it? I think it's like… French or something," he said.

"It's Latin," she corrected in a whisper, breathlessly.

She looked up at him, her beautiful eyes staring right at him, opened wide with surprise and excitement.

"It means: *the Rose and the Thorn meet in Salem.*"

TWENTY EIGHT

Caitlin and Caleb stood in Boston Common, at the top of a small hill, looking out, surveying the park. He held a map of the Freedom Trail which he'd just bought in a store, and he ran his finger along it again and again. Caitlin stood beside him, holding out both halves of the ancient scroll.

"Read it again," he said.

Caitlin squinted to make out the words. She read:

The Four Horsemen travel a trail to freedom.
They leave common ground,
Enter a ring of blood,
Meet at the house,
And find the ones they loved
Beside the fourth tip of the cross.

"A trail to freedom," Caleb repeated aloud, concentrating. "It *must* be a reference to the freedom trail. It would make perfect sense. Its right in the middle, right between Salem and Martha's Vineyard. We're in the center.

"And the 'common ground' reference...that *must* be Boston Common, where we are right now. It would also make sense. In the 1600s, where we're standing, they hung the witches. It is a very important spot, especially for the vampire race.

"The scroll...it says they 'leave common ground.' But that means we *begin* here. I'm not sure why. And the rest of it...'a ring of blood'...'meet at the house,' 'the fourth tip of the cross'...I just don't know where we go from here."

Caitlin looked around again. The view from up here was commanding. There was still some snow left, despite the warming weather, and several kids were sledding down the other side of it, screaming in delight, their parents joining them. As Caitlin looked out, she saw a very beautiful and idyllic park. It was hard for her to imagine witches being hung here.

She surveyed the hilltop, but all she saw was a large tree. There was no clue whatsoever.

"Why 'four Horsemen'?" she asked. "What's that about?"

"It's a reference to the Apocalypse. The Four Horsemen of the Apocalypse, spreading out to the four corners of the earth. I think what it's saying is that, if we don't find the sword, it will bring the Apocalypse."

"Or maybe," she said, "we'll bring the apocalypse if we *do* find it."

Caleb turned and looked at her, deep in thought. "Perhaps," he said softly.

He looked around. "But why *here?*" he asked again. "Why this spot?

Caitlin thought, and something occurred to her.

"Maybe it's not about this place," she said. "Maybe it's about leaving this place. About the journey," she added.

He looked at her. "What do you mean?"

"The scroll talks about traveling, about leaving one place and going to another. Maybe it just wants us to *go* to these places, to travel the road. But not necessarily find things along the way. Maybe it's about the *journey.*"

Caleb furrowed his brows.

"It's like those people who walk those mazes, those Labyrinths," she said. "It's the walking—that's the reason they go. Not the destination. By walking in certain directions, in certain patterns, it's supposed to, like, change you in some way."

Caleb looked at her with appreciation. He seemed to like her idea.

"Okay," he said. "I'll buy that. But even so. Where would we walk? Where would we go next?"

"Well," she said, examining it again, "it says they leave 'common ground,' and enter 'a ring of blood.' So our next stop would be the ring of blood."

"Which is?" he asked.

She stood next to him, and stared at the map. There were 18 sites on the historic freedom trail. Two and a half miles' worth. She felt overwhelmed just looking at it. She had no idea where to go next. She looked at all of them, and none seemed to be in the shape of a circle, or a ring. And there was certainly no reference to a ring of blood.

She read the captions on the map, and still couldn't find anything.

Then, she saw it.

There, at the bottom of the map, was a footnote. Beneath the caption for the Old State House. It read: "At the base of the building, on the street, stands the spot commemorating where the Boston massacre occurred."

"Here," she said excitedly, pointing. "The Boston Massacre. There's nothing about a ring, but that certainly qualifies for blood."

She looked at him. "What do you think?" she asked.

Caleb studied the map. Finally, he looked at her.

"Let's do it."

*

As Caitlin and Caleb left the park, turning down Court Street and heading into the heart of the historic district of Boston, the old Statehouse came into view. It was a large, brick building, perfectly preserved from the 1700s, with multiple historic windows and topped by a large, white cupola. It was stunning in its simplicity and beauty.

As they reached its base, they walked around the structure, looking for the site of the Boston massacre. Finally, as they turned the corner, they saw it.

They both stopped in their tracks.

It was a ring. A perfect circle.

The spot marking the Boston massacre was small, hardly bigger than a manhole cover. They came close and examined it.

It held no special markings. It was just a humble circle, made up of small tile, embedded in the ground at the base of the Old State House.

"It makes sense," Caleb said. "We are definitely on the right trail."

"Why?"

"That balcony, above it," he said, gesturing. "That's where the Declaration of Independence was first read."

Caitlin looked up at the small balcony on the building.

"So?" she asked.

Caleb breathed deeply, preparing to explain.

"The founding of this nation was really the founding of a *vampire* nation. Freedom and justice for all. Liberty from religious persecution. A small group of people conquering a huge and mighty nation. Do you really think a small group of humans could have achieved this?

"It was *us*. *Our* kind. That is what the textbooks won't tell you. The founding of America is the founding of *our* nation.

"But the darker vampire races, like the Blacktide Coven, have tried to hijack our work ever since. That's why there have always been two warring factions. Good and evil. Liberty and persecution. Wherever there is one, there is the other.

"Your father, whoever he was, I'm convinced was one of our founders. The most powerful vampires were. And it is they who held the most powerful weapons, and stored them for future generations."

"Stored them?" Caitlin asked, trying to process it all.

"The sword we're searching for—the Turkish sword—is designed to protect, not attack. In the right hands. In the wrong hands, it can be a horrible weapon. That's why it was hidden so carefully. Only the right people are meant to find it. And if anyone was in a position to hide it, it would have been your Dad."

It was too much for her to process at once. It was hard for her to take it all in, to believe that all this was true. But it did seem to be adding up. And it did feel like they were nearing the end of the trail.

"I don't see any clues here," Caitlin said, looking around.

"Neither do I," he said. "So, if your theory is right, and it's about the journey, that would mean that, for whatever reason, we were meant to just see this, and then continue on the trail."

Caleb took the scroll and studied it again, holding it with her.

"'Meet at the house'," he read slowly. He stood there, thinking. "What house?" he asked aloud.

Caitlin took out the freedom trail map once again.

"There are a lot of houses on this trail: the Paul Revere house, John Coburn's house, the John J. Smith house...It could be any of them. Or it could even be a house that's not even on the trail," she added.

"I feel like they put us on this trail for a reason," Caleb said. "Whatever it is, I feel it must be on the trail."

They both studied the map again, reading all the captions. Suddenly, Caitlin stopped. Something occurred to her.

"What if it isn't a house at all?" she asked.

Caleb looked at her.

"For some reason, the reference to an actual house feels too obvious to me. All of the other clues are much more subtle. What if it's not literal? What if it's figurative?"

She ran her finger along the trail.

"For instance, what if it's actually a church? Look," she said, pointing. "The Meeting House Church. It's just around the corner."

Caleb looked at her, and his eyes open wide in approval.

He smiled. "Glad you're on my side," he said.

✳

They walked quickly down Washington Street, and within moments they stood outside the Meeting House Church. It was another perfectly-restored, historic church.

They entered, and were stopped by an attendant.

"I'm afraid we just closed," she said. "This is a working museum. It's five o'clock," she said. "But feel free to come back tomorrow."

Caleb turned to Caitlin, and she could feel what he was thinking. He wanted her to test out her mind power on this woman.

Caitlin stared at her, locking eyes, and sent a mental suggestion. *She would let them in. She would make an exception for them.*

The woman suddenly stared back at Caitlin. She blinked.

Suddenly, she said, "You know what? You two seem like such a nice couple. I'll make an exception for you. But don't tell anyone," she said with a wink.

Caitlin turned to Caitlin and smiled, and the two of them walked inside.

The church was beautiful. It was another huge, open space, with massive windows in every direction, and filled with wooden pews, all empty. They had the place to themselves.

"It's huge," Caitlin said. "Now what?"

"Let's follow the trail, to start," he said, gesturing at the marked museum trail beneath their feet, the large, red arrows guiding visitors where to walk.

The trail took them to a series of museum exhibits and small plaques, displayed along the wooden railing. They stopped and read.

Caitlin's eyes opened wide. "Listen to this," she said. "'In this spot in 1697, Judge Sewall apologized for being one of the Salem witch judges who, in 1692, condemned the witches to their death."

Caleb and Caleb looked at each other. The reference to Salem excited them. They must be in the right place. All the clues from their search were converging. They felt so close. As if the sword were hiding just beneath their feet.

But they looked around carefully, and did not see any place, any clue that would point them elsewhere.

"Well, this must be the 'meeting house.' And if you're right, if it's about the journey, then the question is: where's the fourth place?"

He held up the scroll again.

They leave common ground,
Enter a ring of blood,
Meet at the house,
And find the ones they loved
Beside the fourth tip of the cross.

"We've left 'common ground,'" he said, "we've entered 'the ring,' and we've 'met at the house.' Now we have to 'find the ones they loved, beside the fourth tip of the cross.' So, if you're right, if it's about the journey, that means we have one last destination."

They both stood there, thinking.

"I think that 'find the ones they loved' is a reference to finding your father," he said. "I think there's just one stop left. But where? What is the 'fourth tip of the cross?' Another church?"

Caitlin thought. She racked her brain again and again. She studied the scroll, then reached over and studied the map. She, too, felt that they were so close. She agreed that there was only one stop left. But it wasn't immediately coming to her. She looked at all of the other churches on the freedom trail, and none of them felt right to her.

Then it suddenly hit her. She took a step back, and looked again at the map. She traced her finger along it, along everywhere they had already traveled. And her eyes lit up with excitement.

"A pen," she said breathlessly. "Quick. I need a pen."

Caleb ran down the aisle, found a pen in one of the pews, and hurried back.

She began drawing a line on the map of the freedom trail.

"It's a pattern," she said. "We've been walking a pattern. We started in the Common," she said, circling it. "Next, we entered the ring of blood," she said, connecting it with a line, and circling it. "Then, we went to the meeting house," she connected that with a line, and circled it.

She held it up, showing him.

"Look at where we've walked. Look at the pattern."

He squinted, unsure.

"It's not finished yet, that's why you don't see it. We've only walked three points. But a fourth point would complete it."

She drew a straight line to complete the pattern.

His jaw dropped as he recognized it.

"A cross," he said quietly. "We were meant to walk in the shape of a cross."

"Yes," she said excitedly. "And if we follow the line, if we complete the cross symmetrically, it only leads to one place."

They both followed the line she drew.

Right there, at that exact spot, at the fourth tip of the cross, lay the King's Chapel burying ground.

"The ones they loved," Caleb said. "The burying ground."

"He's buried there," she said.

"And so, I bet, is the sword."

*

Samantha raced the BMW on the outskirts of Boston, Sam in the passenger seat beside her, heading along the highway towards Salem. She was increasingly annoyed at the growing difficulty in finding his dad. She'd been sure, when she'd seen those Facebook messages, when Sam had told her with such excitement that he'd been in touch with him, that this would be easy. She would just take him to his dad's house, and from there it would be a direct path to the sword.

But things had gotten complicated. She hadn't expected to encounter that creep, and most of all, hadn't expected to develop any feelings for Sam. It was complicating things. Making her less sharp. Her original plan had been so simple: find his dad, kill them both, and return with the sword. Now she wasn't sure she wanted to kill Sam at all. Especially as she looked over at him, and saw that fresh scar on his cheek, the reminder of how he'd tried to save her.

More than anything, she was mad at herself for that, mad at her lack of discipline. She hated feelings. They always got in the way.

After she'd seen his watch, after he'd given her the lead to Salem, she could have easily cut him loose. But for some weird reason, she wanted him around. She didn't quite understand why. She'd told him she needed his help, for something important to her, and that they'd need to go to Salem. Was he game? He'd broke into a big smile. This was clearly a kid who didn't care about going back to school.

Besides, she could still use him to find his dad. That had been a lucky break with the watch. But Salem was a big place. And that inscription could mean anything. Having him around might actually come in handy.

Suddenly, she sensed something, and slammed on the brakes. Their car screeched to a stop in the middle of the highway.

"Whoa," Sam said, slamming his palms on the dash. "What's the deal?"

Several cars screeched to a stop behind them, leaning on their horns.

But Samantha didn't care. She had felt something in the air. A vibration.

She sat there and raised her chin. Sensing.

Yes. There it was again. So close. The signal was unmistakable. There was important vampire activity. Right here in Boston. The vibration of it coursed through her veins. It was so close. She felt an urgency. Maybe, even, something to do with the sword itself.

She suddenly peeled out of traffic, made a sharp U-turn. All the traffic on both sides of the highway screeched to a halt, as she sped down the opposite side of Storrow Drive.

Sam was thrown against the side of the door, as he tried to get his bearings.

"What's the rush?" he asked, surprised, and a bit scared.

Samantha drove another few hundred yards, then made a sharp left, screeching and cutting off four lanes of traffic.

"Change of plans," she said.

*

Kyle jumped off the yacht before it even docked, and landed nimbly on the Boston cobblestone. The Russian soon landed beside him.

He had thought of killing the Russian on the boat ride over, many times, but while it would make him temporarily happy, it wouldn't get him what he needed. So he decided to give him one last chance, to see if he could, this time, point him in the right direction.

If the Russian was clueless in Boston, then he would kill him for sure. And then just find another way. Kyle looked over at him impatiently.

At least the boy still had that big wound on his cheek. Kyle was sure it would leave a nice, big scar. The thought of it made him happy.

Luckily for the Russian, his eyes lit up, and he pointed.

"She is definitely here, my master," he said, excitedly. "I sense her. Strongly. Only blocks away."

Kyle broke into a grin. This time, it seemed real. Yes, he believed him. Blocks away. He loved the sound of that.

Kyle approached a shiny, new Towncar, its driver standing beside the open door.

As they approached, the Russian opened the passenger door and got in.

"Hey!" yelled the driver.

But before he could react, Kyle, with one strong punch, had knocked him back several feet in the air. Without even slowing, Kyle got into the driver's side, and with the car already running, peeled out.

Kyle raced through the Boston traffic, veering for the fun of it and slamming hard into a car as he went. Horns began to blare all around him. He smiled widely. It made him feel just a little bit better.

Within moments, he knew, that sword would be his.

And then he would kill them all.

TWENTY NINE

As Caitlin and Caleb left the Meeting House, turning onto School Street, the King's Chapel Burying Ground came into view. It was only two short blocks away, and a direct, straight walk.

The fourth tip of the cross, Caitlin thought. *It all makes perfect sense.*

As they walked, she marveled at the fact that they had walked, this entire time, in the shape of a cross, as if they had been led by some invisible hand.

Caitlin felt her heart beating faster. She was nervous to finally meet her father, if he was alive. And nervous to see his grave, if he should be dead. She wasn't sure how she would react either way. But she was also excited, relieved to at last know exactly who he was, where she came from. She was excited to know what her lineage was, and what her destiny would be.

She was also nervous that this would mean the end between her and Caleb. What if they really found the sword? What would he do then? Would he go and wage his war? Save his coven? And where would that leave her?

The two of them held hands as they walked towards the graveyard, only 30 yards away. She felt his grip tighten. Maybe he was sharing the same thoughts. Whatever they found in the next few minutes could change both of their lives forever. Caitlin felt Rose retreating within her jacket.

The sun was setting as they entered the small burying ground. The King's Chapel Burying Ground was relatively obscure, the smaller and more forgotten of the two historic Boston burying grounds. It wasn't even all that big, a mere 100 feet wide and just a few hundred feet deep. It was scattered with small, humble tombstones, hundreds of years old.

A narrow cobblestone trail wound its way through, and Caitlin set Rose down beside them, and the three of them walked it together. Caitlin and Caleb scanned each and every stone. Caitlin's heart was pounding, as she read each inscription. Could this one be her father? That one?

They began in the back, at the very last row, and went stone to stone, searching for a clue, for anything. She found herself attracted to the larger stones, the bigger monuments. She had hoped her father would be someone important, whenever he lived, hoped one of the grand monuments would be reserved for him.

But none were. In fact, his name was not to be found anywhere.

As they finished their search, back to where they began at the entrance, Caitlin looked over, and realized that there was one last row of graves. It was the row closest to the street, closest to the entrance. They walked it slowly, stone to stone.

And there, at the very end, it was.

A tombstone: "Elizabeth Paine. Died 1692."

It was the same Elizabeth Paine of Salem. The same woman of Hawthorne's *Scarlet Letter*. The same woman who, Caleb had told her, had mated with a vampire. The same woman who bore Caitlin's last name. This was where she was buried.

Was this who they'd been looking for all this time? Had Caitlin been looking, not for her father, but for her *mother*?

Or was it Elizabeth's husband that was the vampire?

Caleb came close, and kneeled beside the grave with Caitlin. Rose came and sat down beside him, also staring at it, as he examined the stone carefully.

"This is it," he said, in awe. "This is where we're supposed to go. It's her resting place. Your ancestor."

"So," Caitlin didn't know how to begin, "is it my *mom* we've been looking for all this time?"

"I don't know," Caleb said. "It could be that *she* was the vampire. Or it could be the one she wed."

"But," Caitlin began, still confused, "does this mean that they're dead? Or are they still alive?"

Caleb shook his head slowly. "I don't know," he finally said.

He took out the scroll again: "*And find the ones they loved beside the fourth tip of the cross.*" He looked around the graveyard. "This must be the place. These are the 'ones they loved.' This must be the fourth tip of the cross. There is nowhere else it could be," he said, scanning the yard. "Yet I see nothing that hints at where the sword is hidden. Do you?"

Caitlin look around the small yard again, as the sun lit it a blood red. She sighed. No. There were no clues whatsoever.

And then something occurred to her.

"Read it again," she said. "Slowly."

"'And find the ones they loved,'" he read, slowly, "'beside the fourth tip of the cross.'"

"*Beside*," she said, her eyes lighting up.

"What?" he asked.

"It says *beside* the fourth tip of the cross. Not *at* the fourth tip of the cross. *Beside* it," she said.

They both suddenly, at the same time, turned and looked at the large, stone building beside them.

The King's Chapel.

*

As they entered the empty church, Caleb quickly shut the massive door behind them. It slammed with a bang, reverberating. The church was closed and the door had been locked, but he had broken it with his sheer strength. Now they had the place to themselves.

As they walked into the beautiful, small chapel, the sunset light poured in through its stained-glass windows, Caitlin felt immediately at peace. It was a cozy and elegant place, its pews segmented into family boxes and all lined with red velvet. Perfectly preserved. She felt as if she'd stepped into another century.

Caleb walked up beside her, and the two of them slowly looked around. A stillness hung in the air.

"It's here," he said. "I can feel it," he said.

And for the first time, Caitlin could feel it, too.

She noticed that she was beginning to sense things more strongly, and she could sense the sword's presence here. It electrified her. She didn't know what excited her more: that the sword was here, or that she could sense it on her own.

Caitlin set Rose down beside her and walked slowly down the carpeted aisle, trying to use her heightened senses to feel where it could be. Her eyes locked on the pulpit.

At the far end of the chapel, a beautiful, small circular staircase ascended and ended in a pulpit. It looked like a place where ministers had preached for hundreds of years. For some reason, she felt drawn to it.

"I feel it, too," Caleb said.

She turned and looked at him.

"Go," he said. "Ascend. It is *your* sword. It is *your* lineage."

She continued down the aisle, and slowly ascended the circular staircase. Rose walked with her, and sat at the base of the steps. She looked up at Caitlin and watched her. She whined softly.

Caitlin reached the top, a small box, just large enough for a preacher to stand in, and surveyed its woodwork, wondering where it could be. There was no obvious sign of anything, only a wooden railing, as high as her chest, built in a semicircular shape. She felt the smooth wood, aged with centuries of use, and saw no compartment, no drawers, nothing obvious.

Then she saw it.

There was the slightest impression in the wood, something painted over. The shape of a tiny cross. About the size of the cross she wore.

She scratched away at the impression, and years of paint came off. There, indeed, was a keyhole.

She removed her necklace and inserted it. It was a perfect fit.

She turned it, and there was a gentle click.

She pulled, and nothing happened. She pulled harder, and she could hear the cracking paint. The hinges had been completely painted over. She reached up and pulled harder, and scraped away at the paint. She got her fingers in enough to grab a hold of the door, and yanked hard. She could begin to see the outline of a tall, thin, narrow compartment. She yanked again.

And it opened.

Old air, stuck for centuries, came out at her, along with a cloud of dust.

And as the dust settled, her eyes opened wide.

There it was.

The sword.

It was stunning. Covered in gold and jewels from the hilt to the tip, she could already feel its power. She was almost afraid to touch it.

She reached in, and reverentially took hold of it.

She gently put one hand on the hilt, and the other on the scabbard. She pulled it out slowly, and stood, holding it up for Caleb to see.

She could see his jaw drop.

She held on the scabbard and extracted the sword, and with a soft, beautiful clang, the blade was revealed. It was made of a metal she did not recognize, and it shined unlike anything she had ever seen.

The energy coming off of it was overwhelming. It felt like electricity, and was running through her hand and up her arm.

With this sword, she felt she could do anything.

*

Samantha screeched the BMW to a halt right front of the King's Chapel. Abandoning the car in the middle of the road, she jumped out. Sam, following her, jumped out the other side.

Horns blared.

"Hey lady, you can't park there!" yelled a cop, approaching her.

Samantha reached up and brought her fist down on his nose, smashing it and causing him to drop to his knees, unconscious. Before he could hit the ground, she reached out and grabbed the gun from his holster.

Sam stood there, gaping, in shock.

"Holy shit—" he began to say.

But before he could finish, she grabbed him in a chokehold and picked him up off the ground.

Before he knew what was happening, she had him in the air, carrying him up the steps and through the door of the King's Chapel.

"Samantha!" he tried to yell. "What are you—"

Dragging Sam, she kicked open the church door with one foot and raced inside.

"DON'T MOVE!" Samantha shrieked.

Samantha stood there, in the aisle of the King's Chapel, holding Sam hostage with her left arm, and pointing the gun at his temple with her right.

Samantha looked up and saw that girl—Caitlin—standing at the top of the pulpit, holding the sword. Her sword. The sword she needed.

Off to the side, she saw that other vampire. That traitor to her coven. Caleb.

And in front of her, in the aisle, was a small, growling wolf pup.

"Drop the sword," Samantha yelled, "or I'll kill your brother!"

Sam squirmed in her grasp, but his strength was no match for hers.

"Please," Sam said, "don't do this. Why are you doing this?" he whimpered.

Samantha could see that Caitlin looked confused. Unsure what to do. She kept looking over to Caleb, as if wanting his advice on what to do next.

"Don't give her the sword," Caleb said firmly.

"If you don't, I will kill him!" Samantha screamed. "I swear it!"

"Sam?" Caitlin cried out.

"I'm so sorry, Caity," Sam whimpered. "Please. Give her the sword. Don't let her kill me."

A tense silence blanketed them, as Caitlin clearly debated.

Rose began to snarl, heading slowly towards Samantha.

"Okay," Caitlin finally yelled out. "If I give you the sword, you'll let him go?"

"Yes. Throw it down," Samantha ordered. "On the floor. Slowly."

Caitlin hesitated another moment.

Then, suddenly, she threw the sword.

It landed with a clang on the floor, in the center of the aisle. Equidistant between her, Caleb, and Samantha.

At that moment, Rose ran and lunged for Samantha.

And Samantha aimed and fired at Rose.

*

There was suddenly a crash at the door, and in a blur of speed, Kyle and Sergei stormed in.

In the already chaotic room, this unexpected twist threw everyone off guard.

Kyle took advantage of the confusion.

Before anyone could react, he raced down the aisle, and in one blow, he managed to knock both Sam and Samantha unconscious. Her gun went skidding to the floor.

Caleb didn't lose a beat. He raced right for the sword, which was still sitting on the floor.

But Kyle spotted it, too, and was dashing right behind him.

Before Caleb could reach it, Kyle jumped on top of him, smashing him in the back with his elbow, and knocking him to the floor.

Kyle landed on top of him, and the two of them, equally matched in strength, began to wrestle, only feet away from the sword.

Sergei took advantage of the confusion. He raced down the aisle, heading for the sword himself.

Caitlin had initially been too shocked by all the chaos, but now she jumped into action. She had to save Caleb. Kyle was on top of him, gaining the upper ground, and raising his thumbs to his eyes to gouge them out.

She jumped off the pulpit, flying through the air and landing 15 feet below, on the church floor. She raced towards Kyle, and with one blow kicked him hard in the ribs, sending him, just in time, flying off of Caleb.

And then, suddenly, without warning, Caitlin was in a world of pain.

She shrieked, as she felt cold metal piercing her back, her skin, her intestines, coming out through her stomach, then leaving just as quickly.

As she sank to her knees, she could feel the blood racing up through her throat, her mouth, her teeth, dripping down her chin.

In her shock, her agony, she looked down, and realized she'd been stabbed from behind. Through the back. By the sword.

"NO!" sobbed Caleb, as he turned to her, rushing to her side.

Caleb was so distracted, he did not see Sergei, standing over them, holding the bloody sword, pleased at his work, grinning an evil grin.

"You killed me before my time," he snarled down at Caitlin. "Now I have returned the favor."

Sergei suddenly raced off, darting down the aisle of the church.

Kyle scurried to his feet and raced after him, and out the front door.

As they ran past her, Samantha regained consciousness, and in one quick motion, she grabbed a hold of the unconscious Sam, hoisted him over her shoulder, and bounded off after them.

The church was now empty, save for Caitlin and Caleb. And Rose, lying off to the side, whimpering, bleeding.

"Caitlin!" Caleb cried, as he held her shoulders. He leaned over her, caressing her face, and could feel the tears streaming down his cheeks.

He had been too shocked by seeing her hurt to even think of the sword. He knew, somewhere in the back of his mind, that the others had left the building, were getting away, that they had the sword. The sword he had spent his whole life sworn to protect.

But now, seeing her lying there, bleeding, dying, it was all he cared about. Caitlin.

As she lay on her back on the church floor, Caitlin felt the world get so cold. She felt tremendous pain gnawing away at her back and stomach, felt the blood leaving her body quickly, and, dimly, felt Caleb's hands on her face, holding her head.

She looked up and saw the church ceiling. And Caleb. She saw his beautiful face, looking down.

She knew she was dying. But despite everything, despite all the pain, she didn't feel much sadness for herself. Instead, she felt sadness at the idea of not being with him.

"Caitlin," Caleb said, sobbing. "Please. Don't go. Don't leave me!"

He cried as he rocked her.

Caitlin looked up into his large eyes, now a shade of black, and tried to focus on them.

Don't go.

But she couldn't.

"Caitlin," he said, between tears. "I want you to know. I see it. I know who we were together. In our past lives. Now I can see it all," he said.

Caitlin tried to speak, tried to find the words, but her vocal cords were closing up. Her throat was so dry, and the blood was garbling everything. She tried, but it came out in barely a whisper.

"What?" Caleb asked, leaning over close. "Say it again."

He leaned all the way over, putting his ear to her mouth.

"Turn...me," she said.

He stared at her in horror, not sure if he'd heard correctly.

With her last ounce of strength, Caitlin reached up and grabbed his shirt, pulled him as close to her as she could.

"Turn me!" she commanded.

It was the very last bit of strength she had.

As her eyes closed on her, she felt the world slipping out from under her.

And the last thing she saw was Caleb, getting closer, closer, his two front teeth protruding, longer, and longer, as he leaned.

And then she felt the exquisite pain in her neck, as his two teeth punctured her skin.

And then her world was blackness.

FACT VERSUS FICTION

FACT:

In Salem, in 1692, a dozen teenage girls, known as "the afflicted," experienced a mysterious illness that led them all to become hysterical and to independently scream out that local witches were tormenting them. This led to the Salem witch trials. The mysterious illness that gripped these teenage girls has never, to this day, been explained.

FACT:

Nathaniel Hawthorne's most famous work, *The Scarlet Letter*, is based upon the life of a real woman, Elizabeth Paine, who lived in Salem, and who was punished for refusing to reveal the identity of her baby's father.

FACT:

Nathaniel Hawthorne did more than just write about Salem: he was a lifelong resident, and came from many generations of Salem residents. His great grandfather was one of the main prosecutors in the Salem witch trials.

Hawthorne's house is preserved, and it remains intact in Salem to this day.

FACT:

In Boston in the 1600s, Witches were hung on the hilltop of Beacon common.

FACT:

Elizabeth Paine is buried in the King's Chapel burial ground in Boston. Her tombstone is clearly visible, in the first row of graves, beside the chapel.

To view some images of the settings in the novel, visit www.morganriccbooks.com

COMING SOON...
Book #3 in the Vampire Journals

To join the mailing list and be notified of future books, please email:

morgan@morganricebooks.com

Please visit Morgan's site, where you can hear the latest news about the novels, see additional images related to places in the books, and find links to follow Morgan on Facebook, Twitter, Goodreads and elsewhere:

www.morganricebooks.com

Also by Morgan Rice

TURNED
(Book #1 in the Vampire Journals)

CPSIA information can be obtained at www.ICGtesting.com
227036LV00001B/20/P